My Cousin Death

My Cousin Death

MARY McMULLEN

DOUBLEDAY & COMPANY, INC.

GARDEN CITY, NEW YORK

All of the characters in this book
are fictitious, and any resemblance
to actual persons, living or dead,
is purely coincidental.

To my sister, Ursula Curtiss

My Cousin Death

In the First Place

The rain didn't help at all, the morning Paul Kinsella set out on his odd mission. A mission undertaken in rare kindness, which in certain lights could be considered reckless, potentially dangerous, and even fatal in its implications.

The guilt hadn't helped either, while he sat over breakfast, deliberately putting off his departure, and had a third cup of coffee with his wife, Isobel, in the morning room of the house on Fitzwilliam Place.

He had contemplated telling her. They were so close that often she could see inside his mind and heart, and keeping anything from her was not only difficult but painful to him.

But—put yourself in her place. How would he feel if she said to him over her coffee, "I'm off for a few days. An old friend, a man I used to be in love with, is very ill and wants my company as a sort of final gift before he dies. I could hardly refuse him, now could I?"

He would feel betrayed. He would be furious. And he would certainly command her to put away such a mad fancy.

Don't tell her.

Business in Donegal, a knotty matter, perhaps three days, four. "I'll call you when I get the chance, Bel."

She was incurious about the business affairs of Kinsella and Tierne, Attorneys at Law. It was enough to know that it was a solid and even gilt-edged firm, busy, elegant in its conduct, and pleasantly rich. It had been established by Paul's father.

As always he had packed his own bag. Bel had early in their marriage exhibited an air of charming helplessness in dealing with practical daily matters. The one time she had done his packing for him, before they had gone off to Paris for three weeks, she had forgotten all his socks.

A warm robe; it might be cold in the house at Ballybrophy. He hadn't been there for over twenty-five years. Heavy tweeds, a Shetland sweater, four shirts including the challis. Weatherproof English shoes. Pajamas? He never wore them.

"Of course there will be nothing physical in our relationship if you are kind enough to renew it for this little last gasp of time," Amy had said in her letter.

Well, yes, pajamas anyway. Some sort of shield? He owned one pair, ivory silk, given to him by Bel's sister Beatrice for Christmas last year.

Books. There might not be a book in the house; she had never been much of a reader. Seutonius's *The Twelve Caesars* and Trollope's *Rachel Ray.*

In the broad front hall, its walls and ceiling delicately lathered with white plasterwork, Bel returned his good-bye kiss, and dropped her arms slowly and reluctantly as always even when he was only going off to a day's work three streets away. In a direct uncomplicated fashion, she loved with all her heart.

He was a tall man, handsome, dark-haired and dark-eyed, with an open face well disposed to all the world. He had a wide mouth that smiled easily, and a fine Roman nose. Bel was particularly fond of his nose.

She touched it with her fingertip. "You look . . . I don't know . . . a little overhung by interior storm clouds. Will you have a nice comfortable place to stay when you get there?"

Vaguely, "I may or may not be in the house." What house, whose, unspecified. "Let's hope I don't have to bed down in a cow byre. I'll let you know where I can be reached." Disliking himself, disliking the words in his mouth, narrowing his eyes so that, this close, Bel couldn't read them.

His maroon Mercedes was parked in front of the house. Raincoated, he got into it, tossing his bag onto the back seat. What a blessing if it wouldn't start.

And what an asinine childish thought. As if there weren't train connections, buses, cars to be had at hire. The Mercedes did start, at once, and the windshield wipers began to deal with the rain.

Not a gentle straight-down benediction rain, the kind he enjoyed, but an ill-natured heavy slanting from the northeast. Now at ten in the morning, it was dark as dawning, heavily purple. Ominous, the light, or the lack of it.

Ballybrophy, where Amy Veagh lived, was a good seventy miles from Dublin. Not Kinsella territory, thank God. Although when you were up to what some people might say was no good, fate had a way of placing someone you knew smack on the most unlikely scene.

Unfortunate, just for these few days, that his Mercedes wasn't an anonymous black.

Pausing just east of the little town of Kill to let a duck with her winding tail of ducklings cross the rainswept road, he began listening again to the letter. He didn't think of it as words on paper but as a thin soft faraway cry for help, or solace.

"I know this is a most peculiar request, my dear Paul."

He had been at twenty-six not exactly engaged to her, but there was an unspoken understanding in the air about them. He was invited to Ballybrophy summer weekends, along—discreetly—with other young men and girls of his age. But he and Amy were always a pair in tennis doubles, shared the same picnic basket, and when there was dancing were mostly in each other's arms. She was a softly pretty, quiet girl, Amy.

"It seems I haven't long to live, something they call melanoma. There is no cure of any kind. There is just the waiting."

On his twenty-seventh birthday, he had met Bel, the middle one of the three beautiful Mahon sisters of Leam. He had fallen immediately and irrevocably in love with her and she with him. There was one frightful, painful last visit to Ballybrophy, this time no party, just all by himself. He and Isobel Mahon were married in a burst of flowers and candles, family and friends and confettied splendors that all but rocked the little church of St. Agnes at Leam to its foundations.

He had taken it as a matter of course that the Veagh family business would be snatched away from the offices of Kinsella and Tierne. But it had remained there to this day. Amy, without brothers or sisters, was alone after her parents died. When matters of investments, of property, of taxes arose, he and she corresponded by letter or, if necessary, by telephone. She was always quiet and pleasant, as if it had always been he, and she, and never they. She hadn't, he gathered, married.

He had been in contact with her, legal or social, perhaps several dozen times in several decades. There was never any air of the bridling, rejected woman about her when they met. Bel knew her slightly and liked her. In the relatively parochial society of well-to-do Dublin and its environs, it was inevitable that she learn that Amy Veagh and Paul had once been—well, you know, I think she had her wedding dress all but ordered, poor darling. Happy and safe in her love, Bel considered Amy when they did meet as an attractive and thoroughly acceptable might-have-been. If Isobel Mahon hadn't, their very second time dancing, melted deep into the arms of Paul Kinsella.

"You have been the only one, in some strange way always the center of my life. And now to what I want to say. Or ask. I have torn up four sheets of paper trying to get this down, so I will just be direct, not to say naked about it."

It was after eleven by the dashboard clock. He stopped at Naas at a pub where often he and Bel refreshed themselves after the steeplechasing at Punchestown, and moodily drank a half pint of Guinness.

To have existed without knowing it as the ghostly center of another woman's life all these years—the thought scalded him. He was not a vain man and was bitterly uncomfortable on this pedestal, this pinnacle. All the years when he had been so happy with Bel, deep in his work, enjoying and even relishing every day of his life, delighted with his daughter, pleased with his son. But always first and foremost, his whole being an embrace of his wife—

"Will you give me as a final gift say four days of you? Let me have you beside my fire, and across the tea table, and at dinner, and in the woods walking if the rain ever stops. I want your voice and your presence. I want to be sure if I remember the exact shape of your hands."

He had thought about it for three hours and then picked up the telephone. At Ballybrophy, a young woman's voice answered. "Miss Veagh is after having an ulcerated tooth seen to at the dentist's in Roscrea."

"Tell her please that Paul Kinsella will arrive there on Tuesday afternoon of next week."

The report on the dental visit was momentarily reassuring; there was nothing of romance, of wild lost love, about an ailing tooth. She'd be what age now? He was fifty-seven. That would make her fifty-three. Yes, entirely fitting, completely within reason and propriety, a visit to an old friend and client who hadn't long to live.

"If you do come, and please God you will, I want you under my roof, filling my house. I want you across the landing deep asleep. I cannot tell you how safe I will feel and how warm. And how for a time contented. Of course there will be nothing physical in our relationship . . ."

Another voice, probably his own, said in his head, "Did you hear what Paul Kinsella did in April? Told his wife he was off to Donegal on business and went and stayed—secretly—with the woman he was thinking about marrying before he met Bel. Not a quick visit to say a polite hello, but four days."

He was ahead of time in spite of the rain. The softly curving roads were lightly traveled at this hour. In Aghaboe, he stopped again and without appetite ate crackers and cheese and drank the family whiskey, Niall's.

A few weeks back, he had heard a Temperance Society man at a corner on Baggott Street shouting his hellfire at a small straggle of women and elderly men. "The un-blessed Trinity!" cried the man. "John Jameson, Thomas Powers, and Niall's, and the last hasn't got the nerve even to put the Christian name to it! They call it Irish whiskey. I call it bottles full of doom and damnation."

Wanting distraction, he smiled a little at the memory. It was good whiskey, with a disarmingly delicate fist. Every Christmas, the distillery saw to it that four cases arrived at his house, this merry largesse in addition to the annual incomes paid by the family-owned concern to its member tribes: the Nialls, Mahons, Fitzacres, Quests, Parrys, Poyntons, and Blaines, and their connections by marriage.

Not wanting to arrive in the dead and yawning depths of early afternoon, he circled Ballybrophy at random. A pleasant countryside, the Slieve Bloom almost lost in the rain, a remote blue that might have been mistaken for a low-lying cloud. To the left, a lake without a name, small, rain-pocked and chill and gray now, where he and Amy had swum, and then retired to the banks among the kingcups and lain in the warm July sun, holding hands and lazily kissing before attacking their cold roast chicken and the pears and apricots from the Veagh greenhouse.

After a pause, he drove hastily away from the little lake. Explore a lane, study a fine chestnut mare with her foal against her wet-gleaming rump in an apple-treed meadow. Idly calculate the possible market value of a splendid rosy stone house set among oaks on a sweeping hill. Have one of the rare cigarettes he allowed himself, and then another on top of that.

Well after three now. The car seemed to dictate its own pace, a foot-dragging thirty-five miles an hour.

At the two tall granite obelisks on either side of the drive, he gave himself a short lecture. If you're going to do it, do it. Do it right, not stingily, doling yourself out, showing what an inconvenience this is to a busy man.

Committed, and feeling better for it, he drove the car around the side of the house and into a garage whose doors were wide open. He got out, opened his umbrella, went back along the driveway, climbed the side stairs of the terrace, and lifted the knocker and let it fall. A good loud definitive sound of arrival.

He didn't know exactly what he expected, but he could have summed it up in two words: the worst.

Instead, the door was opened to him by a radiant Amy, his hand was lightly taken, and leaving the rain and the wind behind him he was led into her warm, bright drawing room, lamps lit, fire blazing, music playing from another room, Vivaldi, lilting.

"My sweet Paul," she said. "And that's just the one word I'll allow myself. It's said and over. Thank you, and then I won't say that again either. I've been watching at the windows for an hour, nose against the glass—excuse the blurs on the pane."

She looked, if pale, luminously pretty, slender, upright in her soft bronze silk trouser suit. Her short hair was dark and glossy, nature no doubt having been given a skilled helping hand. Pearls in her ears and around her throat, a faint festive perfume floating at him.

"You look marvelous, Amy," he said.

She laughed, a joyous sound. "I'm Elizabeth Ardened to my fingertips," she said gaily. "And I've saved up some new clothes. You have no idea, what fun. First, your room. If you're not wet through you should be. And then tea, early for it but you've been traveling."

He had stayed before in the large bedroom to the right of the landing, but at some time she had done it over and its furniture and carpet and parrot-patterned wallpaper were comfortably unfamiliar. Lamps on here too, books stacked on the bedside table—he needn't have worried about reading matter. Off the bedroom, its own big bathroom, new too, immense tub with fitted sliding glass shower shields, thick white towels on a triple-tiered steam-warmed chromium rack.

Tea was served by the maid who must have answered the telephone, a sturdy broad young woman with warm blue eyes, introduced as Sally Poole. Well, of course, wise of her not to have dismissed for his visit what servants she had; a nice little item for the town of Ballybrophy. "She had this friend to stay, a man, and she let them go for a little holiday, now why I wonder?"

Seeing his eyes follow Sally Poole to the door, Amy said, "There are just she and her husband, Kevin—he drives the car and takes what care he can of the grounds and greenhouse. You can see we're somewhat overgrown. You are plainly and simply an old friend come to pay a visit." The explanation was making her blush. "Occupation not named, place or places of residence not named. Alone here, I do have visitors to stay, often, particularly as I haven't lately been jaunting off to Paris or Florence."

The evening that followed, and the Wednesday, Thursday, and Friday were entirely innocent if taken out of context.

They breakfasted late, on hot fresh muffins and butter and honey, bacon and eggs (Paul) and tea and thin toast (Amy). Lunches were light, prepared by her, salads and fragrant soups, preceded at eleven by a glass of sherry each. Dinners were splendid, the table candlelit and flowered. He ate his food with a partially assumed hunger and hoped that the Pooles, in the kitchen, had genuinely hearty appetites.

The rain did stop, an hour here, an hour there, and they walked in the woods. Rambling leisurely walks, Paul slowing his own vigorous pace. The Veagh demesne composed eighty acres, and there were no neighbors to peer and chat across nearby fences.

"You'll want time to yourself," Amy said. "Disappear, or read, or whatever you want. I'm supposed to nap when I feel like it."

But he did very little disappearing. As always able to put himself vividly in other people's places, he thought, This may be the last view of the pale sunlight hitting the poplars on the hillside in just this misty blued and gleaming way. This may be my very last such fire—a chopped-down dead rose tree sending a poetry of sweetness through the house.

By tacit consent, they went nowhere near the town of Bally-brophy together.

They played billiards, at which she was very good, and he was helpful when she was stuck in her crossword puzzle.

"But you're an active man, Paul, this must be driving you mad."

"Not at all, it's a delightful rest."

Bel was mentioned only once. "How is Bel?" "Very well, thanks." He called her the first evening and said there was no point in giving her a number as he was in and out so much, but he would be in touch every evening at about this time.

Amy maintained, at least outwardly, her spirits. Once when he was rounding the house corner he caught her unaware, leaning on the terrace wall, gazing, her face gaunt, stricken, her eyes wet; a woman in grief, utterly alone. Not seeing him, she turned and went into the house. Ten minutes later she was sparkling.

In front of the fire in the evenings, she told him amusing stories about her eccentric father, and he found tales of the Parrys and Nialls and Kinsellas, interrupting himself with his own catching laughter.

Friday morning they fished in the drizzle, in a noisy crystal-amber stream, and caught four speckled trout which she broiled for their lunch. "Children are right," Amy said. "Make-believe is the most wonderful game in the world."

There were only a few slips, holes in the smooth cheerful fabric. After the hour by the stream he, damp and muddy, went upstairs to shower and came down rosy and brushed.

"Ah, a new man. There's nothing like—do you shower or do you like a two-foot-deep bath?"

Both of them suddenly contemplating the naked soapy Paul, his body still powerful, well-muscled and lean. A curve of desire on Amy's mouth, quickly erased. "I'll just run out and get some fresh parsley. Will you fix us a martini?"

One afternoon, standing beside her in the steamy greenhouse while she picked white grapes, he made himself ask the impossible, the achingly necessary question. "How long, Amy?" "Six months, a year, or any time at all." Her face was turned away from him. "Gather ye grapes and pleasures while ye may—and what a perfectly lovely day I am having."

The Pooles were a mannerly pair and showed no open curiosity about the visitor, whatever their private speculations might be. Kevin Poole, a balding man a good deal older than his wife, stout and bland, took it upon himself unasked to wash and polish the maroon Mercedes Friday morning. "A beautiful job she is, sir."

Sally, passing Paul with an armload of fresh sheets, said shyly, "You've done wonders for her, Mr. Kinsella, she hasn't looked this well for a year."

He came finally to wish that she would break, humanly break. Scream, weep, raise a raging fist at fate, instead of wearing this unreal enameled bravery.

He wasn't sure which was the more dreadful, but on the whole he would have been more at home, toward the end of his stay, with noisy ragged grief.

He had his own tightrope to walk. Far nearer to the earth than hers on high; and she without a safety net. But his was in its way a difficult feat. To be kind without showing the faintest sign of overt kindness in operation. To be open, warm, affectionate, in the face of acknowledged love. To touch when necessary—the hand reaching out to help, crossing to a little island in the stream where she wanted to pick the white violets—without implying an answering cry of the flesh. To be minute-to-minute mindful of the avoidance of any prim conscientious withdrawal—"Remember, madame, that I am a married man."

He was to leave after tea on Friday. "Seventy miles, you'll need sustenance." There were thin cucumber sandwiches, a Lady Baltimore cake (how in God's name had she remembered that when he was young it was his favorite?), tiny tomatoes baked inside airy cheese puffs, chutney toast.

The house, for all its central heating and open fires, was drafty, and in this ghostly blue late afternoon a keen wind was blowing. In the middle of a difficult bite, he shivered.

"I know," she said. "That lovely warm safe snug place you'll be going back to." After her one cup of tea, she poured out a Niall's for both of them.

Oh Christ, he thought, what exit line? What exit face?

She saved him the trouble. She stood up, bent, and kissed his forehead. "I never say farewells—I don't believe in them. I'm going up now for my nap, but a bath first, the running water will help—if I don't hear you driving off, in a way you won't *be* leaving, you'll still be here. For me, you have already left yourself here, so that I can have you always. Just a matter of closing my eyes, and then a bit of summoning. God bless you, my darling."

He found himself standing, too late, reaching out his arms. She was across the room and up the stairs.

He finished his drink in one swallow. His bag had been brought down to the hall. Sally Poole held his raincoat for him. "Safe home, Mr. Kinsella," she said. And, "Thank you," for the five-pound note he slipped into her hand.

At the end of the long straight driveway, he looked back at the house.

There were no lights in her bedroom window.

"Quiet without Mr. Kinsella," Sally said as she was undressing for bed. "Not that he's a noisy one."

Kevin, with a bottle of ale at his elbow, was taking a completed roll of film out of his Kodak. Snapshots were an enthusiasm of his, and he had four albums stuffed with them, going all the way back to his childhood.

"I have a nice one of them leaning on the west fence side by side," he said. "I might have it blown up and framed for a Christmas present for her. If she lasts that long."

"How can you talk that way?"

The Pooles were uncertain of the nature of Miss Veagh's illness but had perceptive eyes and ears and knew there was something badly amiss. The week before Mr. Kinsella came, she had stayed in bed for four days, and had hardly touched her food.

On Friday afternoon, one week after her guest's departure, Amy Veagh was found by Sally quietly dead in her bed. She had not come down for lunch; a tray, tea and toast and consomme, had been brought to her room. It was untouched.

Sally blessed herself. "God have mercy on her." Crying, and guiltily wondering if there would be anything in the will for the Pooles, after her changing it on Tuesday and calling them in for witnesses, she ran down the stairs and telephoned the doctor.

Bernard Lemass, M.D., had been the Veagh family doctor since Amy's childhood. It was he who had diagnosed her fatal illness, demanding at the same time that she go to Dublin for a second opinion. It confirmed his.

He arrived at the house within a half hour. Alone in the big bedroom, he studied Amy's face. He went into the bathroom and checked the sleeping capsules in the medicine cabinet. He had given her a prescription for two dozen of them several weeks back. There were nine left.

He looked about for a note and then thought, No, of course she wouldn't have left a note. She'd have wanted it tidy. Finished.

He was an old man, long accustomed to relying on his own instincts and the decisions he built upon them. Uproar, fuss, scandal —his dear Amy, whom he still thought of as young. And all the Veaghs behind her. She wouldn't at best have had more than a year or a little over.

With a composed face, on which there were a few tears, he signed the death certificate. Cause of death: "Melanoma." In the space provided for any other pertinent information, he wrote: "Expected, at any time."

Shortly after the funeral, Paul was informed by a solicitor in Ballybrophy that Miss Veagh had made a new will dated 23 April 1979, leaving the bulk of her estate to him. The solicitor's letter conveyed a faint but starchy disapproval between the lines. He would know very well that Kinsella and Tierne were Amy Veagh's Rolls-Royce lawyers; that he was only called upon for minor local matters having to do with Veagh dogs accused of killing chickens, or an occasional parking misdemeanor.

The news jarred Paul badly. The date made it worse. She had made the change a few days after he had left her house.

The letter was waiting for him on an evening when he got home after a six-day conference in London. He found that his office had been informed of the death. In the normal way, if he had been at home, he would certainly have gone to the funeral.

Perhaps, under the circumstances, it was just as well he hadn't.

"See that upstanding fellow in the fifth pew? They say his name is Kinsella. He's her lawyer. They say she left everything to him."

"Sure it's a funny thing, but he looks exactly like the man was staying with Miss Veagh just a bit back. Kevin was telling me about him, what a grand car he had, special upholstery, honest-to-God leather to match the outside of the car . . ."

The thought of suicide immediately crossed his mind. And then because it was an indecent probing—and was unbearably possible —he buried it.

One large secret from Bel had been enough. As she came rosily out of her bath, trailing a scent of carnations through the firelit bedroom, he told her that Amy Veagh had died and had left something substantial to him in her will.

"Oh dear God, the poor woman," Bel said with her ready and shocked sympathy. "What of, at her age?"

"I understand that she had a relatively rare form of skin cancer, melanoma, always sooner or later fatal." He still hadn't gotten his breathing back properly.

Bel bent to the fire for life, for warmth.

"It was kind of her to leave something to you," she said, "but why, I wonder? I can't remember if she had any family or not. And of course she never married . . . a mystery to me, she was a very pretty woman."

"I can only imagine," Paul said, standing at the window, his back to his wife, "that she had no one else, really, in the world."

In the Second Place

One

Nobody has to have three reasons for anything, Conor Niall told himself on the way to Ireland.

One, he was very tired and hadn't had anything like a real vacation for almost a year, and his work had sent him to so many towns and cities in the United States that he swore he knew every crossroads. A change was sorely needed.

Two, he was very fond of his Aunt Bel—never admit fonder even than he was of his mother, Ivy, the youngest of the Mahon sisters. Paul Kinsella had died very suddenly of a first and final heart attack a year and a half ago, and he hadn't seen Bel since the funeral.

Third, in Bel's letter thanking him for the splendid Hermes handbag he had sent her for her birthday, the paragraph: "Sara Parry is here, staying in the cottage. I think you met her when you were last here. She's working on something for Telefis Eirann, a play, or more properly a teleplay I suppose. Like the man who came to dinner, only in reverse, she came to pay me a call, and I asked her to dally here for a while, I am fond of Sara. Too early to say, but I think she and Fitz might make a pair, they seem quite pleased with each other's company."

In the time it took to finish the rest of the long letter, now only vaguely taking in its details, he not so much decided as apprehended that Sara Parry was necessary to his life.

The idea had been flickering around him for some time, but he had been too busy and usually too far away to do anything about it.

Every seat on the Aer Lingus 747 was occupied. In spite of the size of the plane, this induced a feeling of claustrophobia, of being caught and hemmed in by a crowd you couldn't get out of.

Asking for a scotch from a passing liquor cart, he murmured to the hostess, "Do you have any way of disposing of legs? Tossing them out of the emergency exit or something?"

The hostess smiled and dimpled. Now where had she seen this man before? She wasn't sure, but he must be Somebody. His voice, low as it was so as not to disturb those already slumbering, seemed not unfamiliar either.

He looked like a man for whom, on the part of Eire's national airline, it would be appropriate to do a courtesy. Maybe he'd tried for a good seat and been too late. He didn't look short of money.

"There's an empty seat in First Class," she murmured back, close to his ear. "I'll bring your scotch up there when I've finished the aisle, will I?"

Conor was a man people did do favors for, but he was nevertheless grateful and pleased. Not one to wave aside the unexpected blessing, he settled himself in the wide comfortable chair and started on his scotch, observing with objective interest that the man across the aisle was drinking Niall's Irish Whiskey.

He was, without being what he would call somebody, known by face and voice in a vague passing sort of way to millions of American viewers of television news.

Working as a reporter for the New York *Times* had more than contented him until he was spotted, at a cocktail party, by a man from NBC.

At the idea of entering television journalism, he felt at first an embarrassed and embarrassing return to gangling, blushing adolescence, wanting to shuffle his feet, "Aw gee, *me?* Me, on camera? Me, in black and white and full blazing color?"

But he was adventurous by nature, and none of the foot-shuffling feeling showed in his many interviews and auditions. His reaction reports were more than favorable. "Class, style. But not in my judgment off-putting to the proletarian eye. See Utley, Jennings, etc." "Voice good. He doesn't *sound* like a news guy, but maybe that's a plus." "Yumyum. I mean, projects attractiveness." (He was never shown these collected comments and would not have liked them, but was at the same time perfectly well aware of the partially cosmetic nature of casting the evening news. More or less the same stories to tell, on the three networks; the viewers' choice of which network to look at boiling down to who there was covering the story.) "Hey kids, in the words of the old movie studio days, we may have a PROPERTY here!!!"

Kindreth, who still had a nagging belief that news should be news, not an exercise in entertainment, a horse for advertisers to ride, scribbled, "An intelligent, able, and seasoned reporter."

With an early natural taste and ear for languages, he was at ease in French, Italian, and Spanish, and could hobble along reasonably well in Greek and Russian. This didn't hurt him at NBC either.

The money talked about was better than his *Times* salary and could, he was told, go up and up. Well, it was a different world today, and if you didn't give it your wholehearted stamp of approval and weren't entirely at home in it, there wasn't much you could do about it. He liked and admired Edwin Newman, Roger Mudd, David Brinkley, Morley Safer, and in his heyday Eric Sevareid, and looked with amused awe at Walter Cronkite, who had replaced Dwight Eisenhower as the American Father. He realized that a few spoken sentences from such men had far more reach and influence in terms of watching and listening millions than anything written by the kings of the op-ed page of the *Times:* Reston, Wicker, Lewis, Baker.

Why not? said Conor Niall to himself, and took the job. When he offered his resignation at the *Times,* his immediate superior, Jessup, said, "I understand navy-blue mascara photographs blacker than black. With this helpful piece of advice I will wish you luck and farewell."

Sara was in Hollywood while all this happened. She had hesitated about going, but he had said, "Sara darling, you may not get a chance like this again. *Go.* It will only be for a couple of months, after all. I'll fly out and see you."

The man across the aisle pressed the bell button over his head and when the hostess came ordered another Niall's. Seeing his unoccupied gaze, as one on the edge of launching into conversation, Conor hastily opened his paperback and gave every evidence of being buried in Joyce Cary's *Herself Surprised.*

He was mentally rereading Bel's letter, which he had gotten three weeks ago. He had decided not to tell his aunt that he was on his way to her. Sara might cut and run.

Droppers-in, unannounced, especially from three thousand miles away, deserved to be boiled in oil, but never mind that.

"Sara Parry is here . . . I think you met her."

More than met, even that first evening. In the drawing room, the dining room, full of people; their two pairs of eyes looking at, or looking for, each other.

I must not be separated from you.

The closed glossy black coffin at one end of the drawing room, the steady candle flames, a great bowl of roses on a nearby table, nothing more of flowers. An immense gathering of family, aunts and uncles, cousins, and nieces and nephews, the usual funeral gloom and the repairing merriment, a hum of voices as in a theater lobby during intermission.

His Aunt Beatrice introducing the two of them. "Surely you must have met as children? She's your, let's see, second cousin once removed or is it the third and not removed at all . . . oh dear, I give up."

Beatrice looked tragically beautiful, taking over for Bel, who would not and could not appear for more than one terrible half-hour. "Of course, she adored him . . ."

Sara had been spending her Christmas vacation in Ireland when Paul Kinsella died. After the funeral, Conor persuaded her to change her departure date by one day, and they returned to New York side by side in the Aer Lingus plane; and a good part of the way, hand in hand.

Their love affair began immediately and naturally; or had already begun by the light of the coffin candles. She was twenty-eight, he thirty-three. It was by no means a passing fancy, just for fun.

They lived, Sara said, in each other's pockets; more literally, in her pretty apartment on Murray Hill while his own three rooms on West End Avenue slowly gathered even more dust.

She was working in the television department at Mall and Mall and, when time could be taken off from love, was writing a script she thought might make a one-hour television play. It might and it did. CBS bought it.

"Oh God, everything is too wonderful to be true," Sara said. "Especially you."

She quit her job to devote herself to free-lancing scripts. "After all, there's that nice Niall's money we get. I won't starve for a while."

Through Henry Duckworth, a photographer-director she had worked with in television, and who was now what reviewers described as that dynamic young director, she got an offer to do the screenplay for a book she loved, Mrs. Gaskell's *Cranford.*

"Dynamic usually means making a lot of noise and wanting your own way," Conor said. "But you're not terribly easy to trample on."

"It won't jam your coffers and it won't make you famous, but you can get your feet wet," Henry Duckworth said. Adding with the euphoria so headily to be breathed in Los Angeles, along with its fumes, "But who knows? Maybe a blast, maybe a killer."

Telephone calls from coast to coast were better than nothing, but not much better. In any distress, and there were plenty of distresses, she wanted him desperately, and when something good had happened she wanted him even more, to share it with.

During the three months, she flew East twice, he West once; snatched sweets that did not satisfy but only taunted the appetite.

When he called to tell her about his new job, she said how marvelous. "But dear God when now will I ever see you? Except standing there dark and dear on the screen?"

"That's a case of the pot accusing the kettle," voice a little dry.

Cranford laid an expensive egg. "There wasn't enough beating and killing and blood," Sara said. "Or more accurately, there wasn't any of it. The high point, sexually speaking, was Miss Matty rolling her little red ball under her bed to see if there might possibly be a man hiding there." But her screenplay drew forth admiration from several influential critics' tongues. She resisted doing the second film Henry Duckworth offered her. Now, however, Conor never knew from day to day where he would be, when. Caught up in the drive of work, they had begun, inevitably, to seem a little unreal to each other.

Evenings by her fire, in Murray Hill, deep nights, breakfast together by the window overlooking the back gardens of houses on East Thirty-eighth Street—had all that ever happened?

On impulse, and not having been able to reach Conor, who it seemed was on his way back from Nashville, Tennessee, she flew East for a third time in the middle of the script for "Don't Cry

Baby." She worked as hard and steadily on the plane as she would have in her office.

Getting in at close to midnight, she called his apartment on the off chance. Oh lord, the classic situation, so commonplace it shouldn't have been a surprise, a deadly shock. The girl's voice, a little above a whisper, "Yes, he's here, he's asleep, he's exhausted. Who—?"

"A cousin passing through, nothing important," Sara said.

Conor half waked at the two rings before the bedside phone was snatched up. The girl had deliberately hidden here when the party of nine or so went on to dinner. He had found her in his bed when he came home. Oh well.

"Who was that?" he asked.

"Some man. Drunk out of his mind. If it rings again, let's not answer it."

Sara had what she thought at the time was a hysterically funny vision. He bolting upright in bed, clutching the sheet to his comely bare chest and shoulders, staring into an unseen camera, the tousled pretty girl naked beside him, and saying in his decisive sign-off way:

"Conor Niall, NBC News, New York."

She spent a wide-awake night at her own apartment. In her closet, she discovered a pair of moccasins of his, polished and in mint condition, and hurled them down the incinerator in the hall. Then she took the ten o'clock plane back to Los Angeles.

Well, she thought, grimly burying herself in work, it happens. Dismiss it. Dismiss him. There were lots of men around whom she hadn't much troubled to look at before. She was astonished and taken aback to find in her bones, flesh—genes? early religious training?—an absolute and infuriating physical constancy.

Wouldn't it be awful if she turned out to be like her cousin Bel? Only one man for Bel, forever.

Nonsense.

Well then, go ahead and prove it.

Whenever he called, manners or pride kept her friendly and pleasant. This didn't work for long.

"What in Christ is wrong with you, Sara? You sound as if you were addressing someone at the other end of the conference table."

"I'm sorry, a dreadful rewrite staring me in the face—you were great covering that murder at the U.N. I must, *must* go to work now."

If they had been in the same city the air would probably have been cleared by one face-to-face furious battle. Conor saying, "What d'you think I am, a Trappist monk?" And more; he was an articulate man. Then peace, and laughing at herself—old-fashioned Sara still wearing an invisible dark blue Peter Thompson convent school uniform. But they were separated by three thousand miles.

In spite of its horrible title, "Don't Cry Baby" was a runaway success that startled everybody. Sara had a remarkable gift for comedy that was unexpectedly warm and kind in this harsh decade, and was invited to undertake a third screenplay. I don't know, thought Sara. The juice seems to be drained out of everything. I'll call Conor and ask his advice. No, I won't.

Was he thinking of her now as someone he had semiofficially taken on—a burden, a responsibility?

She was making a lot of money and doing too many things and seeing too many people. If I'm not careful, I'm going to start to look a little battered, she thought. Or feel it.

Assigned to Los Angeles for an epic fire in Beverly Hills consuming quarter-million-dollar houses by the dozens, Conor went to see her one evening at her elegant little house near Hermosa Beach. It was full of people.

"Hello, you sweet strange lovely man you," said a dark girl while he was hunting Sara. "No—not strange. I saw you on TV right after someone cleaning plaque off dentures. You poor love."

In the kitchen, he discovered Sara. For a few seconds there was no one else there. He put his hands on her shoulders and bent and kissed her in a puzzled, exploring way.

"Take your hands off my girl," a man said behind him. He turned out to be Hank O'Malley, millionaire's son, entrepreneur, producer of the moment, mainly famous for backing the smash rock musical, *Potty*.

Not seeming to pay any attention to that, Conor, however, asked a little later, "Are you his girl?"

"I'm nobody's girl," Sara said. "Last I heard I was my own."

They were standing in the hall, clear of the crush. Hank O'Malley came up behind her, put a forearm under her breasts, and began kissing the back of her neck.

She pulled sharply away, toward Conor. She looked pale and younger than she was, and smilingly desperate. But smiling about whom? Desperate about whom?

This was no time to find out. He could see the tawdry headline: "NBC Newsman in Bloody Combat with Millionaire Producer at Cocaine-Whiffing Beachside Bash."

O'Malley had disappeared. "I must leave," Conor said. "Plane to catch." He made no attempt to conceal his anger and impatience, his boredom with where and how he was.

"Good-bye then. I'm sorry you had to go out of your way to . . ."

"Go our of my way? To see you? And are you ever coming back East?"

"If I did, you probably wouldn't be there, would you. One way or another, you wouldn't."

A final meeting of the eyes; a rising fury in him he couldn't define. What was she saying, what was she accusing him of? A dirty Irish trick, this verbal diving into mist, into mystery.

He said an abrupt good night and left. That was in late October. He hadn't seen her or talked to her since. It had not been a casual relationship and could not end casually with a little sighing whimper. It ended with a bang.

One evening, the evening of her birthday, in February, he happened to be in Murray Hill, on foot. Someone had told him she'd seen Sara Parry the night before, at the Ginger Man. "Didn't you and she once . . . ?" He went into a florist's and bought two dozen yellow freesias. The square white box swinging by its cord from his finger, he turned in under the canopy of her building.

No need to press her buzzer, three other people going in at the same time. He went to 3G at the end of the carpeted hall and his fingertip was an inch from the bell when, quite near the front door —he must be in her little kitchen, the man—a voice said, "Well, happy birthday, my darling." The sound of a cork being festively drawn. Then silence.

Conor turned away, went down in the elevator and out under the canopy, and threw his freesias into the wire trashbasket handily waiting on the curb not ten feet away.

Several months later he heard that she had left Hollywood and was in Paris, working on something or other for the BBC. Yes, anywhere, my dear rover, except Murray Hill and West End Avenue. But now you're pinned down, placeable on a map. Now you're in Leam.

He had gathered from Bel's mid-May letter that Sara was not at present on the wing. It was now the first week in June. Attention wandering from his book, he directed it prudently toward the window, across a plump woman fast asleep. In Dublin, hire a car. Take care of his arrangements for borrowing Telefis Eirann's cameras and a crew. He had an open-ended assignment, for the "Today Show," a wander through Irish pubs. And there was his cousin Jerome to see, and drink with. Say a day and a half in Dublin, and then to Leam.

The engines of the 747 were a kind of soporific, but the man across the aisle was still not ready for sleep. "One last Niall's," he said to the hostess. "Or make it two, don't like to bother you again."

Conor thought an ale might be just what he needed for sound slumber. The drinks arriving on the same tray, his would-be conversational partner crashed the barriers.

"Pardon me, but you look like—who? A model maybe?"

"No."

"Well, everybody has their double. Even I do." As he was balding, stout, rumpled, and undistinguished, the qualifying adverb seemed unnecessary.

"This Niall's. Great stuff. Ever tried it?"

"On and off, yes."

"A friend of mine knows a member of the family that makes it. Her name's not Niall, now what could it be?—Sara something. He's in the movie business, cameraman. Classy-looking girl, he says. I asked him if he could get a case of the stuff off her, for me. Never hurts to try, does it."

"I think she and Fitz might make a pair."

"No," Conor said, finishing his ale, snapping off his overhead light and closing his eyes. "It never hurts to try."

Two

"Well," said John Upshaw, pausing for a moment before crossing the bridge. *"Well."*

He hadn't been at all sure what to expect. Money around somewhere, he had hoped and thought. But in his experience you could, in a family, have a well-to-do aunt and turn around to find a cousin in an old dress with the hem coming unstitched, up to her shins in dusty bobbing chickens.

Romantic wasn't a word in his vocabulary, but it seemed to him that Leam House looked like something out of a story. It was hexagonal in shape, built of creamy pale stone with slate roofs, a ring of long windows straight down to the brilliant clipped lawn. A great clouding and murmuring of trees at the sides and back; beeches, willows, poplars. The house was set in the center of a courrab in a round, still, shining body of water somewhere between a pool and a lake. Close enough to the water that from where he stood he saw its shimmering reflection.

All right, it could still be mortgaged to the doorstep for all he knew. But the matter was worth a try. Oh, very much worth a try.

Especially since he had lost his job as a bus driver in Dublin; drunk at the wheel once too often. Coming along the coast from the city of Galway, he had given a passenger's severe study to the driver of his bus. Fellow had had a drop or two, no doubt about it. If things didn't work out maybe the Galway branch would take him on.

He was, in his own words, dumped in Costelloe. The town of Leam was not on the bus route. Two miles, he had had to walk. Two miles away from the sea, northwest into a green and pleasant pocket strewn with little lakes.

The dusty trudging had somehow been emphasized by a man sweeping imperiously toward him on a horse, passing him in a racket of hooves and limestone dust. What was a Chinaman doing in a place like this? Why on horseback? Or—did Chinese have mustaches?

To look at his ease and perfectly at home in his surroundings, he lit a cigarette before he crossed the stone bridge spanning the water between the long drive and the house.

To his left, at the water's edge, a wink of sun piercing the clouds gave a few incandescent seconds to tulips, flaming rose inside and frosty lavender outside, muscari burning the air with its blue, and smooth and folded at the lapping edge a duck, cream and brown, its head as blue as the muscari. Then the sun went in.

He marched to the front door, white, paneled, flanked with Ionic columns in bas-relief cut into the stone, and raised and dropped the knocker, a heavy ring of shining brass.

He saw someone passing, pausing, at the long closed window on the right, and then the door was opened with a grudging carefulness.

The woman he found later to be Mrs. Broth looked him over. Again.

She said pointedly, "We have the other entrance at the rear—we're not restricted to the use of the fine front door."

She was a tall woman, close to six feet, with a commanding posture and powerfully colored red hair billowed out and up in some mysterious fashion, a pompadour of sorts, around her long melancholy fleshy face. She wore a man's heavy tartan kilt, a bright blue wool cardigan, high-laced sneakers, and around her neck a black ribbon from which dangled a lorgnette.

This she now picked up and held to the bridge of her nose as if to further elucidate the puzzle of why this man had seen fit to turn up at the front entrance.

"Oh, come on, come on," he said. "I have business with Mrs. Kinsella." He dropped his cigarette end on the broad slate walk and ground it under his heel. "Upshaw, John Upshaw, Dublin. I have family news for her."

It had been a quiet morning if not actually dull, and in Mrs. Broth's breast curiosity fought distaste.

"She's out, not expected back for a while. Now where shall I put you? Unless you'd care to wait outside?"

"With the chill in the air and rain any minute? I'd hate to disappoint her—" He half turned.

"All right then, follow me."

Somewhere, she thought, where he'd be under her eye, not given a chance to go sniffing around and perhaps pocketing valuables. She chose the big butler's pantry and brought a chair from the kitchen for him to sit on, leaving the door between open.

From the round table in the center of the kitchen where she was kneading bread dough, she studied him between her hearty slaps and punches. Thin and short, with unhealthy-looking pale-sallow skin, oddly flat mud-brown eyes under extravagantly long lashes. Forty, as near as made no difference. Oily dark hair parted and combed in a schoolboy way, but balding on top. Rumpled suit of some synthetic, dull blue-gray with an unfortunate sheen. Dusty scuffed brown shoes. And the general allover look to her of wanting a good scrubbing.

Did he walk all the way from Dublin then? The shoes looked like it. She totted up the sum total of what his apparel must have cost and placed it—and his—value at about twenty pounds. At the outside.

Mrs. Broth lifted her mound of dough into a floured bowl and covered it with a tea towel. "You wouldn't want to pass along your family news to me? That way we needn't detain you. No doubt, whatever line of work you're in"—a strong glance at the shoes—"you're a busy man."

There was the sound of a car's engine somewhere near the kitchen windows, and then the engine was cut. A calculator by nature, Upshaw mentally sketched another bridge at the rear of the house—if a more or less round house could have a rear—and another drive, another entrance to the property, leading to it.

The kitchen door was opened and a tall blown-about woman came in.

Upshaw got an impression even in that first glance of a drifting gracefulness, a face he vaguely connected with a gilded frame. He did not and could not, eyes flickering, nerves tight, take her in all at once.

He had been frightened about meeting her before he saw her, in the sense that she was going to be his object, his victim.

If you studied the walls and strength of a garrison and figured up their arms and ammunition, you might possibly never dare to attack.

"A Mr. Upshaw to see you, Mrs. Kinsella," Mrs. Broth said in a manner that faintly suggested apology. "There before you, in the pantry."

Upshaw had not been wasting his time while parked on his chair beside the glassed-in cabinets. He had once in his younger days worked as an under-gardener at Powerscourt and, on good terms with the cook, had become familiar with costly plate and china. Stacks and stacks of china here, edges gleaming with gold. Row upon row of drinking vessels, unmistakable, the silent diamond blaze of Waterford crystal.

The sight helped to restore his sagging courage. On the mention of his name, he got up and said, "A private matter, Mrs. Kinsella."

"All right, come along." Bel Kinsella was incurious, only hoping he wouldn't be a nuisance. He looked a little like a nuisance.

Eyes darting, assessing, he followed her, the juices of his appetite flowing increasingly. Twelve-foot ceilings, every doorway double-doored, the white panels gadrooned in gilt. Upshaw had been born in a one-room lodging over a shop.

A great crystal bowl of blue hyacinths and white tulips here, a wall of leather-bound books there, a fire half seen, gracing and warming a room with no one in it. They went into what he supposed was a sitting room on the far side of the marble-floored entrance hall with its angling carved snow-white stairway, its arched window on the half-landing, a peacock in delicate stained glass spreading its tail in the center of the arch.

Bel closed the double doors. Surely not a bill collector? Fitz was in charge of money and was quite good at it.

The room was small and comfortable; but its soaring ceiling and long windows looking into tulips below, willows above, made it seem larger.

Courteously, she said, "Do sit down."

What an odd way he had of moving, walking: a glide. Odd way of talking, too, a sibilant voice that gave the slight effect of a lisp, an insinuating confidential way about it.

"Thank you, I'd rather stand. Been sitting a long time on the bus, and then just now in the pantry."

A watery ray of sun struck his hand grasping the edge of the mantelpiece as though for support. She noticed the long boniness of it, the yellowish skin, the dirty fingernails.

"It's about your husband, Mrs. Kinsella."

The hand in the ray of sun was from that moment forever fixed in her mind.

"My husband is dead, Mr. Upshaw."

"I know." As an afterthought, "Rest his soul. Well, I heard this story about him quite some time ago and forgot all about it. Until one night, a few weeks back—"

Bel's heart action felt a little peculiar. In her soft voice, she said, "I'm not accustomed to discussing my husband with strangers."

"—until, one night, a few weeks back, this fellow and I were having a jar or two and fell into talking about an item in the paper. This woman it seemed died and left half her money to the Pope—in Rome, you know—and the other half to her dog. After we had our laugh, I said, 'I'll tell you a funny one about a will, money left. Funny in a different way.'"

She thought the man might be mad or partly on his way to it. She rose from her chair. The servant's-bell system had long since ceased working, but all she had to do was walk out the french window.

"Needless to say, I mentioned no names, and names need never be mentioned at all if we can come to an agreement." His initial hopes had been modest. Perhaps two, three hundred pounds to quiet a little, inconvenient scandal. This figure had been slowly and steadily rising from the time he crossed the bridge.

"Agreement about what?"

"About your husband and this woman Amy Veagh."

There was no guilty start on her part, no change of color, no sudden narrowing of the eyes.

Something about her expression, between puzzled and surprised, told him she knew nothing about it, nothing at all. So much to the good, so much infinitely to the good. But feel your way; this was unexpected, a bottom stair missed, startling your spine.

Perhaps never was an attempt at extortion, an act of intended crime, so often and captiously interrupted.

A brisk knocking at the double doors and then one half was opened. Mrs. Broth while obviously, in the manner of a police-woman, examining Upshaw and what business he might be about, said, "Will you want the veal roast for tonight or should it be saved for Fitz's birthday, that's Saturday and it's his favorite."

"Oh, Saturday, yes."

"Mozart's Symphony Number Nineteen is on, I forget what key —E-flat? I got it by mistake in the kitchen, but I thought you'd not want to miss it."

Bel went over to a small radio in the bookshelves and snapped it on, turned the dial, and found her Mozart.

A dull flush came up under Upshaw's stale skin. He raised his voice as the door was closed.

"He went to see her, Mr. Paul Kinsella did. It wasn't put about by her to her staff"—he liked the sound of that, "staff," it made him sound familiar with the ways of large houses—"where he had come from, what his profession was. He stayed close to a week."

Bel heard him and did not hear him; it was only later in a corner of her brain that she recovered every word, intact. She found herself intent on the music, and thinking on the surface about Fitz's birthday. Six or so for dinner? Or would he want to go off somewhere with Sara, just the two of them.

There was Sara outside the window now. The rain had started again, but she had her usual look of standing in light. Eyebrows raised, she jerked a questioning thumb westward, toward the town of Leam. Bel opened the window latch.

"Anything you want?" Sara asked. "I'm going in for stamps."

"Yes, get me some. Two pounds' worth. Do I expect you for lunch or are you working?"

"Working, but thanks." She gave Upshaw a mildly curious look and vanished.

Upshaw drew a long breath. "Then, a week after Paul Kinsella left this Amy Veagh's house, she died. In the meantime, before she died, she changed her will. She left all her money, or the bulk of it anyway, to him. It turned out he was her *lawyer*."

Detached as her spirit was strongly dictating to herself to be, Bel felt in her sitting room the distant beginning of a storm—a darkness, a pressure, a vein-squeezing menace.

It had been seven, no, eight years ago. Paul had been, where was it? in London, a conference. And the evening he came back—it was startlingly vivid. The fragrant bedroom fire, and she just out of her bath, and he telling her that Amy Veagh was dead and had left something substantial to him.

She couldn't recall exactly when she had sat down again, but here she was in her chair. The telephone at her elbow rang. There were two telephones in the house, this and the one in the kitchen. When she picked it up she heard Mrs. Broth say, "Yes, she's home."

"Hello, Fitz." Paul Fitzacre Kinsella, her son, thirty-three years old. "Let's not have any truck with Junior, or the Second," her other Paul had said when his son was ten months old. "Fitz ought to do. Particularly as now inspired by him on his back, howling and shaking his fists." It would have been nice if he was here at home. Or would it?

"I'm expecting an Arab, Mamood's his name, there about four," Fitz said. He was at the moment in Dublin. "Hold him for me, will you? Give him tea. He's interested in Carrowkeel, and he wants to see the horse in person."

"An Arab," Bel repeated carefully. "Carrowkeel." Fitz always gave his horses the musical names, or combinations of names, of obscure Irish towns.

Upshaw wondered if this was some kind of code, a summoning of help to deal with him, get rid of him. He waited tensely for several minutes, smoking a cigarette. But nothing happened.

"Yes, all right," Bel said. "Miss Veagh was my husband's client. She left him money. Why are you here?"

"Look at it this way." He held up one finger. "Isn't it funny he wouldn't be announced as her legal man?" Two fingers. "And he'd never been there to visit before, not in the five years the staff had been with her." Three. "She didn't use *his* services to change the will, but called in the local solicitor. Now, why all the secrecy of it?"

Bel stared bemused at his finger. The little finger went up to join them. "And—a married man with a family. Her *house* guest. She a single woman. No one else at all in attendance. The Pooles, the staff, had their own quarters over the garage. She wore her best clothes, and her jewels, and perfume at any and all hours."

"Well, you know I think she had her wedding dress all but ordered, poor darling."

Before going to London, Paul had been off to Donegal for the better part of a week. Not, it seemed now, Donegal, but Ballybrophy, in County Offally. Where Amy Veagh lived. Before she died.

She felt her world dangerously slipping, sliding.

But what earthly reason was there to believe this man? It might be a shabby net of lies, including the great dark lie Paul would have told her, if this other story was true: That he was going to be in Donegal while actually, and secretly, he was staying—living—with his first love.

In her bewilderment and distress, she almost missed the thumb, the fifth statement, going up; the palm now held upright, as if threateningly, at her.

". . . if the heirs she knocked out of the will—they're in the States—ever found out the circumstances, there'd be the mother and father of a court fight. Bringing disgrace and shame on the family, and on the firm of Kinsella and Tierne, who're still thriving last I heard. It so happens I know who they are, the people who missed out."

Silence. Upshaw coughed. "Broken into as we have been, there are points I may have left out. His license number was seen and remembered, at the Veagh house—"

There was a commotion in the hall. The door had been left a quarter inch ajar. It burst open and a large standard poodle leaped in, fresh from a grooming. A prime apricot, the coat tight as crushed velvet on his back, the legs paler frothy pillars of fluff, the crown softly imperious, the nose long, shorn, and regally pointed.

He dashed to Bel's chair and flung himself upward, his trimmed paws with their cropped nails on the flowered chintz arm.

"Well, hello Peach," Bel heard herself saying. "Don't you look beautiful."

The poodle gazed at her with ardent love in his olive-golden eyes and then slowly turned his head to regard Upshaw, standing in front of the hearth.

He tensed and began a soft deep-throated growling. A rare sound from this amiable animal.

"It's all right, Peach." She put her hand on his head, warm cushiony depths of cashmere. "This gentleman is—" Her pronunciation precise and icy.

Is what? A man come to blackmail me, a destroyer, a deadly enemy, Peach. That's who this gentleman is.

Unless I can think my way out of it, get matters straight, *prove* my way out of it.

How?

Three

Bel dropped her hand from the dog's head and put two fingers under his collar. "I think we'd get along better without you, Peach." She opened the door and gave him a light shove out.

Get along where, to what?

The clock on the mantelpiece said it lacked two minutes of noon. All this time, it had been ticking away, measuring as though perfectly normal the seconds and minutes of this darkening midday of June.

Without thinking her way to it, she adopted for herself the role, easy to assume, of the confused and helpless woman, coming a little to pieces in the face of any crisis; accustomed to masculine support, advice, and strength.

The softer, vaguer, even stupider she could seem, all her edges blurred, the firmer she might force him to make his own outlines and character and demands.

"I don't know, it's all so . . . I'm afraid you'll have to let me think about it for a while. When I *can*." She put the back of her hand distractedly to her forehead.

At fifty-seven, she was a beautiful fifty-seven. There was no attempt to dismiss or camouflage the years. Her long narrow face would be as finely planed at seventy, with its delicate aquiline nose, great deep-set violet eyes under sculpted lids and arched eyebrows, its records of laughter, thought, grief, and sheer time. Her hair, in which white mingled with the original pale gold, was center-parted over a high innocent forehead and worn in a soft chignon at the back. The skin of her face and long throat was a warm ivory. She wore no makeup and needed none. Her fluting mouth was the tender pink of a cat's nostrils.

Upshaw, who had been on and off trying, in the way of business, to assess the possible value of paintings, mirrors, furniture,

carpet—that waist-high blue-and-white jar, was it Chinese? between the windows looked as if it was worth plenty—thought she
could have taken a little more care with her clothes, and spent a
bit more on them. White shirt like a man's, the sleeves rolled to
her forearms, thin gray tweed skirt with a cigarette hole, brown-
edged, near the hem. Bare legs. Sandals with mud on them.

"What exactly do you mean by, for a while? I have no money
and no accommodations. I'd meant to leave here with a nice check
in my pocket."

He was pleased with her confusion, her look of being absolutely
unable to cope with him. He added, "And the matter for the time
being taken care of, between us." With a conspirator's look that
said, "Who knows for how long? Who knows how much I'll want,
and when?"

He had adjusted his demand figures upward again, well upward.

Twenty minutes back, she had considered calling the Garda.
This man, who had turned out to be a nuisance as expected, easily
and quickly gotten rid of, led away no doubt shouting threats over
his shoulder.

Or, it might be like dropping a lighted match into a can of
kerosene.

"No accommodations. Oh dear . . ." She ran her fingers
through her hair. "There isn't a hotel, but I believe Mrs. Halloran
just on the other side of the post office takes in people at very
modest rates."

"I'm not leaving this house until we come to an understanding,"
Upshaw said, the almost-lisp pronounced, the flat statement made
the worse because spoken in a cautiously lowered voice. "Here I
am and here I stay."

Granted that she had decided against calling the police, and
hadn't had him thrown out of the house the moment he stated his
business, it was in a topsy-turvy way safer for her, for all of them
—for Paul—if he was in the house.

She had visions of him giving into temptation and beer; and
regaling, this afternoon, the other customers in the bar behind
McCane's, Fancy Groceries, with his story.

"Let me see . . . you're a distant cousin, very." Loathesome to
join in his scheming. But necessary. "You're staying here for a day
or so."

A guest of the house? Without being aware of it, he smiled to himself, a small malicious curve of the thin-lipped mouth.

"And will I have to change my name then?"

"No. Yours will do." What was it? She was horrified to find she had completely forgotten his name.

It was all very well to look and sound as if one were coming apart, but one must not actually *do* it.

Upshaw. That was his name.

She became brisk. She handed him over to Mrs. Broth. ". . . a cousin I haven't seen for, oh, twenty years. He'll be with us for a short time." Sit down and lunch with him? Never. "He's very tired and will take a tray in his room, the one at the far end of the hall —I think we expect Beatrice, don't we?"

"This house," Mrs. Broth said, "is a railway station." She was used to an infinity of relatives, most of them in their own ways attractive. This one, she thought, was the bottom of the barrel. She was glad to show him into what had once been a maid's room when there was a maid; small, clean, but in no way fitted up with luxurious comforts.

All but ordered to remain there, and feeling he might as well ride with his luck just now, Upshaw sat down in a shabby little chair slipcovered in faded daisies. "I'm hungry," he reminded.

A tray indeed, snorted Mrs. Broth to herself. She could see him carrying one, but not being served anywhere and at any time in this fashion. She made him a sandwich of cheddar cheese, omitting mustard, butter, or pickle. As a relish, she added two ancient radishes from James's greenhouse, guaranteed to scorch the throat, and a few stale potato crisps she had meant to give Peach. She thought about tea for him, and thought about beer instead; and ruthlessly discarded both. We don't want him to think he's staying at the Ritz, do we? A paper napkin would do him.

She planted this repast on top of the dresser. He was standing at the window with his back to her. Reckoning up the worth of the property like as not. From here he would be able to see, beyond the water, the roofs of the stable, and perhaps one or two of Fitz's horses for which he got such sinful prices. Once in a blue moon, that is.

"Mrs. Kinsella says you'll want a nap," she commanded, and left him.

Bel forced herself to sit down and eat lunch, which when there were only a few of them was served at the round table between the windows in the library. If she didn't, James probably wouldn't, and he needed his food, especially now. Never strong, and with a heart much more openly tricky than his brother Paul's had been, he was just three weeks out of the hospital after bronchial pneumonia.

Paul had once said to her, "If anything ever happens to me, Bel, God save the mark, take care of James, will you promise?"

Paul had gotten all the pith and vigor of the family. James was thin, almost slight, always holding himself very erect as if to stretch his just-above-medium height. He had clear shining bright blue eyes in a narrow face which was deceptively ruddy-pink and fresh from his work in the gardens. His hair was a soft silky mixture of brown and gray, neatly arranged; he wore a small mustache under his well-shaped Kinsella nose.

Now fifty-three, he had never married, and they all suspected why. A love he couldn't have, near and immensely out of reach.

Bel had made herself insist, after Paul's death, that he close up shop at his apartment and come and live with her. His health had forced him to retire from Kinsella and Tierne. As he had, like Paul, a modest private income from his mother's estate—and unlike extravagant Paul, handled it carefully—it was no problem when the house in Dublin was given up and sold, and they went to live permanently at Leam.

It had been Bel's home as a child and a young girl, and for a fifth wedding anniversary present Paul had bought it for her. The remaining Mahons accepted the money with glee; knowing that they could come and go and enjoy themselves there exactly as they pleased. But not responsible any longer, thank God, for the plumbing, and the gardens, and the bad place on the stable roof.

Mrs. Broth, after giving Bel an examining look, said, "A nice lamb chop. Fortunately under the circumstances small, and that means both of you. Creamed potatoes." She and Bel took turns preparing lunch. "And how long did you say that fellow your cousin planned to be with us?"

"What fellow your cousin?" James asked.

Be careful. James, quiet as he was, often seeming invisible, was extraordinarily perceptive. She had instantly decided, from the moment he entered the library, not to tell him about Upshaw's purpose in coming here, about any of it, at least not now. He had adored his brother, and the shock and distress, or even the leaping fires of rage, might get to his delicate heart.

"Perhaps not quite cousin. An aunt of mine, step-aunt I suppose you'd say," deliberately obfuscatory, "large family of her own when she remarried. In and around Skibbereen, last I heard of them—oh, years ago." To Mrs. Broth, "A matter of a few days, I'd think."

Without being aware of it, Mrs. Broth was readying herself, and the house she loved, and the people in it, for some unnamed trouble.

Just the faintest clues picked up by her lively antennae: something not quite right, shifty, about the man upstairs. A look of having won something, a bet, a race, surprised on his sallow-pale face. The ungentlemanlike obedience with which he had sat on his chair in the pantry, instead of saying, "In my cousin Bel's house I'll sit wherever I choose, thank you."

And Mrs. Kinsella looking not really here, and barely eating. Normally she had a light but reliable appetite at this time of day.

Well, the best *she* could do was to make it as uncomfortable for him as possible, behind the scenes. That might help to speed him on his way. If he complained to Bel, she could fall back on her familiar lament that the house was far too large for her to take care of, and her familiar threat that her sister in Skerries would soon need taking care of.

Wanting to get away from James's considering gaze, Bel drank her demitasse rapidly and then went up to her bedroom. The treehouse, Fitz called it. The upper ring of windows around the house were nine instead of eleven feet tall, but, floor-length, they contributed a remarkable airiness and depth to the five good bedrooms. Her windows looked into the branches of beech and willow, a shifting and murmuring of green that dappled the white walls in sunlight, tinted them with their leaf color in grayed soft air or rain.

When she closed the door, delayed shock hit her. Her knees wanted no part of their responsibility to support. For occasional late-night tête-à-têtes with her sisters Ivy or Beatrice, when they were visiting, she kept a bottle of Niall's in the white double cabinet, painted with faded tulips, under the white-marble bathroom counter. She poured herself a generous portion, sat down by the window to drink it, and told herself that the time had come to think.

She knew she was by nature a great waiter and time-bider, a head-turner and veil-drawer, a follower of the school of Something Will Turn Up. And that she was in a sense spoiled, having been taken care of by men all her life, her self-protective instincts rusted by the warm surrounding strength and love.

But something must be decided, something must be done, right away. He was there overhead, now; not a figment, not a bad dream, but a living, breathing being.

Her first, knee-jerk instinct was to throw up her hands, tell Fitz, and let him handle it. But Fitz's temper was precipitate. If he didn't physically injure the man—calling forth a fury of loud immediate revenge—he would march him straight to the police. Story told again, to amazed and eager ears. Inquiries made, publicity, talk spreading. License number checked, time seen, checked. But stop, *wait*. Paul hadn't *done* anything to Amy Veagh, she died at least a week after he left her house. It wasn't in any way a police matter on Paul's part. Where the Garda entered into it would be to charge Upshaw with blackmail, have him tried and found guilty on Bel's evidence, and put him in jail.

"Now, Mrs. Kinsella, if you'll repeat for the court this story the man approached you with—"

Repeat for the court. Repeat for the court reporter. Repeat for the world.

Mr. Paul Kinsella, having informed his wife that he was going to Donegal, went secretly and instead to stay with Amy Veagh in her house. Yes, just the two of them. Amy Veagh was not only a client of long standing but was the woman he had been thinking about marrying before he met Bel Mahon. Right after his stay with her, Miss Veagh changed her will and left him pretty well her entire estate. And right on top of that, conveniently died.

Mutters of undue influence. Of a lawyer of previously spotless reputation taking advantage of a woman doomed to her death; and he in possession of exact knowledge of the disease. And the secret visit with all its other overtones: the renewal of an old and cherished love.

She could lie in her teeth about that, say she had known where he was those four days, that he had told her all about it in advance. But she couldn't lie away the will.

At the least, a perfectly frightful scandal, personal and professional, for Paul Kinsella and his survivors. An unanswerable and final dishonoring, most especially for him.

At more than the least, if there could be any more than that total scald—Upshaw's reference to Amy Veagh's ousted heirs in the United States. A thunderous court battle. Massive reparations demanded and awarded?

How could she know the heirs were real, true? How did she know any of it, any word of it, was true?

But if it was all invented, how had he had the confidence to come here, to her, without accommodations and without money? "I'd meant to leave here with a nice check in my pocket." He didn't look like a subtle mastermind, a daring schemer. He looked shabbily, patiently, sure of himself.

If a search for the contradictory, the lovely innocent truth were conducted, the search itself would raise all kinds of possibly sleeping questions in people's minds. "You know, I always wondered about that will. And now why at this late date is the Kinsella woman going about asking questions?"

What questions could be asked, and of whom? Amy Veagh was dead. Paul was dead. She had no idea where in Donegal he was supposed to have been, or who his client there was. Unless he had something amusing to tell her, he left his work behind him on the doorstep when he came home.

A nice check. What constituted a nice check? "For the time being," as Upshaw said.

She had no accurate idea of what the family finances were. She was vaguely aware that there was sometimes quite a lot, and sometimes a rather low ebb when Fitz had to pay out large sums for horses he wanted for breeding purposes. Her Niall money came in once a year, and some other source yielded quarterly checks. The handling of money confused and bored her, and shortly after Paul's death she had asked Fitz to take over.

There was never a question of his skimping her, or watching how she spent money. She kept a modest checking account—"No point in kissing interest good-bye," Fitz said—and whenever there was something wanted that the checking account couldn't measure up to, it was hers for the mentioning. *Quarterly*. There might be something in that. Tell him she was strapped at the moment and couldn't even consider writing a nice check.

One hundred pounds? Five hundred? One thousand? Or on up, way on up?

To even offer the putting-off excuse meant that she and he had formed an understanding. Oh, my God.

She considered her two sisters, but only briefly. Ivy, although she lived in a charming villa in Provence with her second husband, the sculptor Marcel Bonner, claimed to be perennially broke, and just three weeks ago had borrowed three hundred pounds. "I can't ask dear Conor, I got fifteen hundred off him in January. You'll have it back as soon as I get my whiskey check." Beatrice? Beatrice had all along been disturbingly a little in love with Paul. What an upside-down delight it might be for her to find out that after all he had been—or a man named Upshaw said he had been—not only unfaithful but very profitably so. No. Not Beatrice.

Cruel, brutal to tell James, and anyway what could he possibly do about it? Telling Fitz would start a chain that might eventually circle your own throat and tighten and strangle you. Sara Parry? She'd probably end up telling Fitz, people close to each other found secrets very difficult to keep. And she might tell him anyway, in concern over his mother's dilemma.

My insoluble dilemma, Bel told herself in a naked freezing flash. But no, there's a way out of everything. Isn't there?

Her daughter Monica was in Iraq with her husband, an engineer with Aramco; and was within a month of producing their first child. Leave Monica alone.

No, don't, can't, tell anyone. Look away from the fleeting idea that it might be her own vanity and hovering pain that stopped her. Paul and Amy Veagh—"My dear, didn't you *know?* They'd been seeing each other on and off for years. Very privately of course." No, never. She could feel the beating of his heart and read the circulation of his blood in his veins across a room. To say nothing of the eyes, which spoke to her before he opened his lips.

Never.

An enormous drowsiness threatened to overcome her. Surely not the whiskey? She had a good head for drink. She fought to keep her mind active and on course. What—until a way was found, or thought up, out of this swamp—was to be done with Upshaw?

He couldn't be kept a prisoner in his room, caged, fed on schedule like a zoo animal. He would have to be allowed to emerge, and be explained as casually as possible to Fitz and anyone else who might and would turn up at the house.

For heaven's sake get it straight and keep it that way. Skibbereen, a step-aunt's family by a previous marriage, her husband had died of—what? Appalled, she realized that she would have to have a conference with Upshaw to get the script settled on, with him.

But she wasn't, really, committing herself to anything by this. Let him think she was a woman in panic, not knowing what she was doing from minute to minute. Not accountable for her peculiar secret plotting with him. No bargain made or signed, just a smoke screen thrown up while she considered matters.

He'll be here at breakfast. At tea. At dinner.

She found herself stalking the room. When had she gotten up from her chair?

Who, now, was the caged animal?

Four

The Arab, Mr. Mamood, had not been in the house for more than twenty-five minutes when he offered Bel a quarter of a million pounds for the property, inclusive.

(Later, Fitz asked, "Were you to be thrown in as part of the deal, inclusive? I must say he was very much taken by you.")

As Bel was a little late coming down, or perhaps the Arab slightly early—none of the clocks could come to an exact understanding with each other—James shyly took over as temporary host. Mr. Mamood showed an immediate and anything but shy curiosity about and interest in the house and strolled, white garments flapping, diagonally across the ample square hall and through the open door into the library.

With the air of a shopper, he cast his eyes over the room-circling shelves and said, "You have no doubt the works of Shakespeare, Austen, Dickens, Dostoyevsky, the Greeks? All the major poets, though I cannot like Chaucer. The man Lewis? *In Wonderland.* Most especially, *The House at Pooh Corners,* our little copy is raggedy."

"Yes, no doubt," James said. "Now, the drawing room is over this way."

Bel had summoned Sara Parry to help her with her guest. "Work or no work, this is one flag you must rally round." With the intention of aiding Fitz in the sale of Carrowkeel to this exotic tycoon, she had asked Mrs. Broth to do her best with tea. All foreigners seemed to expect the Irish to consume their tea around a merry fire, so a fire was lit in the drawing room, and the tea table and biscuit stand were well laden.

Sara, thought Bel, added greatly to the decor, and Mr. Mamood appeared to think so too, obviously torn in which direction to send the strongest gusts of admiration. Her bell of pale loose hair catching the firelight; light plunging deep into her tilted eyes, glowing on the folds of the long cherry-red wool skirt, twinkling back from the gold links around her slender throat, stroking the creamy silk of her shirt.

Upshaw, after some hesitation, took a tall straight-backed chair to the right of the hearth.

Bel, on waking from slumber which had finally, temporarily, rescued her, had had no time for her conspirators' conference with him. She knocked on his door. When he opened it and began, "Look here, I had a sleep and I needed it, but how long do you expect—" she cut across him and said, "Tea downstairs, a guest, here on business. You are as mentioned a cousin and your family is from Skibbereen."

Upshaw washed in the small maid's bathroom. He carefully brushed the scurf off the collar and shoulders of his jacket, reknotted his tie, and took a wad of toilet paper to dust off his shoes. Then he was ready, as he put it to himself, to enter the *en famille*.

He was casually introduced to the little group by Bel. Sara's only immediate reaction was that everybody had at least one unattractive relative.

When he sat down, he started off by worrying what to do with his feet and hands and eyes, but he soon saw that no one was paying any attention to him at all, beyond easy politeness. Famished after his long-ago sandwich and spongy radishes, which even now were burning somewhere in his digestive tract, he helped himself liberally from the biscuit stand, which was conveniently beside him, and gratefully swallowed his first cup of tea.

He did not and could not take a lively part in the fireside conversation, as he had little information and no opinions on the semiscandal at Buckingham Palace, the ruinous state of things in Rhodesia, the race for the American presidency, or the love letters, just published, of the queen of Russian ballerinas.

The weather in Eire was finally gone into. "You rain a lot," said Mr. Mamood, fingering his damp headdress. He had arrived in a white Rolls-Royce and been attended to the door by a chauffeur with an immense umbrella, but the moisture had gotten through all his expensive barricades. "But," gazing at Bel, "so wonderful as they say for the complexion—the woman's."

Bel wished Fitz would hurry up. When you got to the weather

you were almost out of available chat material. In welcome response, Fitz appeared. He entered the room with a sort of silent clang, as did anyone of Mahon blood: a mute, unintentional, but ringing, "I am here."

He sent Sara a quick private smile, and she o'd her mouth in amused admiration at his splendid going-to-Dublin tailoring, more accustomed to seeing him in work clothes or tweeds. "Up to here in mud and manure," as Fitz said. An outdoor all-weather life kept his fresh taut skin red-brown. He had dark red close-fitting Grecian-curling hair, warm bright brown eyes, and a slim straight powerful body. He was easy and soft in his manners, perfectly at home right away with Mr. Mamood, nodding a pleasant greeting to the cousin he had never met or even heard of before, getting down to his tea in a hurry.

"I haggled myself hoarse in Dublin, but I got him, eight months old. You may be familiar with the sire, Mr. Mamood—Sevillion, Spanish, came in third at Ascot last year, but in my opinion he was badly ridden. Sorry I'm late—you'll want to see Carrowkeel."

"Perhaps if we wait a little the rain will stop," Mamood said, obviously relishing his food, drink, comfort, and company. He had just bitten into one of Mrs. Broth's Tidbits.

She had invented these mainly for herself, and turned to them in times of stress or celebration in the way another kind of appetite would have suggested a pull at the nearest bottle of spirits. One Tidbit, two Tidbits for her were all right, James had been heard to observe, but they were a kind of Richter scale; if she sat down to ten it would surely mean the end of the world was in sight.

The creation now being consumed consisted of a square of hot buttered toast furnished with a cucumber slice decked with caviar, and on top of all a rich spoonful of apricot preserve just whispering of curry and sour cream.

"Where do you buy these? Or who is your cook? Are there by chance any more?"

Sara went rapidly to the kitchen and snatched out from under Mrs. Broth's very nose a plate of three Tidbits. "Never mind, Mrs. Broth, I think he wants to purchase you. You'll soon be installed in a silk tent with eunuchs bringing you wine and alabaster jars of perfumed oils."

Three, James thought, looking at the plate. Why three? Is she really bothered about something?

Mrs. Broth's private collation had no sooner been disposed of when the sun came out. Warmly and without any kind of stint; a whole-hearted payment for past misdemeanors. Mr. Mamood looked in wonder at the colors leaping to life all over the room, as the fire paled. Light from the breeze-ruffled water around the house floated high and low, a delightful rippling decoration. It was like being at sea, but upon a very quiet never-never sea. Flowers were emblazoned, early roses burning cream and faintest pink on one corner of the tawny golden marble mantelpiece. Watery radiance sprang from mirrors. The deep-lidded bottomless blue dreamer's eyes of Bel's mother, Clare, on the wall to the left of the fireplace, smiled deathlessly on them all, on the grospoint carpet patterned with pansies, on Sara's face dappled with the shadow of rose leaves, the cobalt-blue sheen of Fitz's tie, the scuffed toes of Upshaw's shoes.

"Well then, now Carrowkeel," Fitz said.

"How pleasant it will be to see him in sunlight." Mr. Mamood looked at his fingers, took a linen handkerchief to them, and sighed with remembering enjoyment. That last one—black walnuts in something made of grapes, Roquefort and bay, insouciantly laid on an impossible alien crisp cracker: matzo.

Bel went to the door with them. Sara had stayed behind, with a signaling light touch on the shoulder from Fitz that said, "Soon."

How, Bel wondered, could she put her request without sounding rude. "Fitz, whatever is decided in your international bargaining, will you save it as a surprise? Remember tomorrow's my birthday."

Her birthday was not in June, but in April. Accustomed to family codes, Fitz said, "All right. No, really, Mr. Mamood, I don't think we'll need your car, it's only a matter of a thousand yards or so."

It wouldn't do at all to have him come back, a half hour, an hour from now, caroling for all the house to hear, "Break out the champagne. Guess what—seventy thousand pounds!"

Sara went to the kitchen to apologize to Mrs. Broth for the peremptory robbery. That was all right, Mrs. Broth said, she had made do with anchovy toast. In honor of the occasion, she wore instead of her kilt and laced sneakers a bright pink knitted suit and ancient highly polished black shoes, the kind Sara used to associate as peeping out under nuns' hems. Sitting at the table sipping her before-dinner sherry, she was in a conversational mood.

"That Upshaw." Her long face grew even more melancholy. "When I think of the people who surge through this house. Your own brother in April with his beard and his bare feet—"

"He's only twenty, he'll get over it."

"—although a sweet boy, a way about him. Have a glass of sherry, do. Fitz's poor wife's aunt, composing poetry in her bed and making me listen to it when breakfast was brought! And Mr. Fitzacre, at his age, with that young girl he said was his nurse, and she not even knowing how to heat his milk. And your Aunt Beatrice's niece by marriage, practicing her piano four hours a day till the whole house was driven crazy, and Mrs. Kinsella made up an excuse to go visit Mrs. Tierne in Dublin. But this *Up*shaw." She snorted. "Plain Shaw more likely, then thinks to give himself a boost and pastes on the Up. Do you ever have premonitions, Sara?"

Mrs. Broth, who had been with the Kinsellas for twelve years, was a sturdy user of first names, except in the case of Bel.

"Yes," Sara said. She had one right now and wanted to get away and think about it. It had nothing to do with Upshaw, but with Fitz's hand on her shoulder, sending her the most specific message yet.

"He's not wanted here by Mrs. Kinsella, you can see that. Then why does she have him? Is this a home for the indigent?"

Sara left these rhetorical questions in the air and took herself to the small stone building across the bridge in front and to the right, almost invisible from the house in its coppice of beeches. It had been built seventy years ago as a studio for a Mahon who fancied himself a sculptor, then revised into a sort of cottage to accommodate family overflow.

In the small but tall living room which still retained its immense out-of-scale casement windows facing north, she lit her own fire and sat down in front of it with the glass of sherry she had skipped in the kitchen.

Well, let's see. Paul Fitzacre Kinsella, thirty-three or so. Irish country gentleman, breeder of racehorses, but in no sense a provincial, not in this family. At ease with books, music; at home in Paris or Rome.

Married at twenty-five, widowed at twenty-nine. His gay reckless Elaine, insisting on going to a party in Killaloe when he was flat on his back with his broken leg in traction. Driven home late along the foggy coast road high over the sea by an inebriated young admirer; a head-on smash with another car; the long plunge into the Atlantic. There had been no children.

She thought he was not a man for casual dalliance. He did not appear to take his religion very seriously, but tradition was deep in his bones; stability, continuity.

Now look. She had only been here a month. But there was something eerily domestic and settled about eating breakfast with a man who was obviously, sharply interested in you. Perching on a fence watching him on a horse. Sitting with him on the grass in the sun surrounded by James's flowers, snatching a cigarette even though you were trying to give them up. ("It's hard in Ireland," she said to Fitz. "Everybody smokes here." "Put it down to a belief in the immortal soul," he explained. "The sooner we're hustled out of this life, the longer we'll have to spend in eternity.")

Only a month. It had taken only three or four days, with Conor. And she as precipitate about it as he. *You are my own.*

That was then, Sara said silently to the fire. This is now.

It was nice here, in Ireland. She loved the mysteries of the weather, the deep peace in which to work. No crash and clatter of ambition, your own and other people's, bursting around your head. A time after great confusion, after losing your way, to browse upon who you were and what you wanted, and what after all you didn't want. A bath for the spirit, leisurely, cleansing. Leaving aside these self-based considerations, she was very fond of Bel, had a special love for gentle James, and not only enjoyed Mrs. Broth but had written her into her script.

Hand on her shoulder. "Soon." Soon what? Oh well, Sara, for God's sake.

If there was something joltingly familiar about him, all right, perfectly natural. Families do have certain resemblances. Above and beyond the resemblances—the sudden amused brilliant gaze from under the angular eyebrows, the cadence of a voice heard a room or so away—Fitz was very much and excitingly himself.

Yes, I lost my way. But now I'm step by step finding it again. She looked down at her tightly locked hands in her lap and made herself loosen them. What were they all about, the hands?

It was time to start thinking about dinner. Would Fitz be hungry as well as thirsty when he arrived? She felt on her face the beginning of a smile and inside her ribs a warmth that had nothing to do with the fire. Yes. It's lovely here. Of course I'll stay.

"And what brings you to this part of the world, Mr. Upshaw?"

After the party scattered, James was left alone with his new cousin. He wanted badly to read his *Irish Times,* he yearned for its pages. This morning had been too busy, in his greenhouse and outside it.

Upshaw, sated with food and brimmed with tea, nonetheless eyed a large portion of chocolate cake on the biscuit stand and picked it up.

"Couldn't pass by without saying hello to the family, distant though we may be." Having invented his destination for his wife, it came readily to his tongue. "I'm on my way to Ballycastle, a new post, manager of a feed and grain store if we can get together on a few small details."

"That must be interesting work," James said politely, his right hand lying itchingly on the *Times* flapped over the arm of his chair. "Would you care to have half the paper?"

"No thanks. This offer to Mrs. Kinsella—a quarter of a million pounds—surely she doesn't want to sell?"

What strange eyes the man had, James thought. They seemed to pick up no light from the fire's blazing.

"Oh no. I believe these people have a lot of money they don't know quite what to do with. It's as if you or I were to offer say half a pound for a particularly fine new variety of tulip bulb."

Bel returning had paused outside the door for a few seconds, listening. In a way it would be marvelous if Upshaw would take matters into his own hands, tell James before she could stop him. Then she would have a companion. Then she wouldn't be alone.

Upshaw on his part gathered that James Kinsella knew nothing of the reason for his visit; nor did that young lord-of-the-manor bastard. Whenever the purported cousin came to his notice at all, a moment or so here and there, he had been absent-mindedly pleasant, bent as he was on his business with Mamood.

From the doorway, Bel said—not having been given his first name—"Well, Cousin Upshaw, shall we have our little family chat? We'll leave James to his paper."

He followed her into the sitting room, where at midday he had laid it all out for her.

"I have been thinking things over." Her voice was as she intended it, untidy, high, a little breathless. "You'd have to show me documented proof. And, just at this time I happen to be flat broke. My checks or whatever they are come in quarterly—and of course I have no idea what sort of money you're thinking of. *If* you could produce documented proof, that is."

"I have witnesses to call on, a photograph of the two of them, the license number, the name of the heirs in the States, the name of the solicitor called in to change the will, and the date of the new will," Upshaw said. This time he omitted his finger count.

"A photograph?" Now genuinely finding it hard to breathe.

"Yes. Would you care to see it?" He took an envelope from his inside breast pocket and pulled out a black-and-white snapshot. "I'll hold it, just in case." Moving in a leisurely fashion, he held the photograph under the light from the lamp beside her chair.

Two people, leaning on a fence, late afternoon watery sunlight striking their faces. Amy Veagh, radiant, smiling, emanating from the 4″ × 4″ square of glossy paper some kind of joy. A joy perhaps more intense, piercing, because it was secretly snatched. On Paul's handsome face, pity or sorrow, tenderness, love? A look which whatever it conveyed also pierced. He was wearing his camel's hair Norfolk jacket. She had given it to him for his birthday two weeks before his journey to Donegal. "How did you know, my darling, that I always wanted a camel's hair Norfolk jacket?" It made the photograph as authentically timed as a date stamped on the back.

Five

It was dizzily like being at a film in which the director had employed special effects. The photograph, blurring as it enlarged, filled the screen, the room, the world. She felt that if she listened hard and watched closely, she could see Amy's hair lifting in the breeze and hear Paul's voice. That close, their heads communing at three-quarter angles to each other's, his voice wouldn't be loud, but low and soft.

The immense picture went back to size. It was the room that was swelling and blurring, it was Upshaw looming like a pillar. But not a tall man at all, seen in the correct focus. If anything, under middle height, and thin.

She was aware that she was in some psychological half-faint and took a hard grasp on the arms of her chair. He was putting the picture away now, into its envelope, tucking it inside his rumpled jacket, lovingly close to his heart.

Any idea she had of carrying it off airily, saying to him that on thinking back of course she had known where Paul was, that week, was now down the drain. She saw herself, through his close gaze, all too clearly.

What a bonus for him. He couldn't possibly have known beforehand that she didn't know. An oyster hauled up from the depths with a nice big unexpected pearl inside it.

"Here, are you all right?" Voice almost alarmed, a hand on her forearm. She noticed in a detached way that he had cleaned his fingernails.

"Yes. And where did you get that photograph?" And what did *that* matter?

"That would be telling, wouldn't it. But I bought it, and I own it, for the time being." It had been well worth the five pounds counted out for Kevin Poole, who was fairly well awash in Guinness, also paid for by Upshaw.

The other details, simple enough when you put your mind to it. A visit to the solicitor, Daniel McGuigan. Sorry to take up your valuable time, sir, but I'm distantly connected with the Veagh family. God rest that poor woman's soul. I'm off to the States, and I was under the impression there was a relative or so over there— I'd like to get in touch with what's left of the family. McGuigan, grudgingly, as though information was money handed over free, gave him the name. Had no idea of where he, or they, might be now but when last brought to his attention living in Bridgeport, Connecticut.

The faint faraway buzzing in Bel's ears stopped. What would a distraught, hysterical, cornered woman do now? She would utter some feeble threat, that woman would.

"If my son knew what you were up to here, I wouldn't like to answer for the consequences, physical or otherwise."

"Oh come, he can't do a violence to me in front of a houseful of people. And anyway would you like him to know about his father?" This indignant concern for the feelings of a son might have been comical, and wasn't, in its deadly accuracy. "The whole point of a secret is that it is kept a secret and not spread here and there. Might as well put it on the front page of the newspaper."

One of the french windows was slightly open. James appeared in it, the late sunlight rimming him in brilliant gold.

"I thought," he said, "I'd just put out a few rununculas before dinner. Do you think you'd like them down by the water close to the path?"

James never interrupted anybody in anything. James never asked her opinion about his gardening. This was his own fine, polished art. Dear James, you're worried for me and you don't know why.

If worst came to worst, she might say to James that she wanted a sum of money, never mind for what. But she had no idea how much money he had at hand at any given time. And the mysterious request might jar, shock, jolt him; lie on him like an illness. No, that would only be a last resort.

If appealing to him was the last resort, what was the first?

Someone ought to at least frighten this confidently attacking man, make him think twice of the possible dangers he might be letting himself in for. On second thoughts, shaken, he might even be attempted to abandon the whole project. She couldn't do it.

Trahey moved, heavy-footed, into her mind.

Fitz's lefthand as well as righthand man, trainer, unofficial vice-president of the Kinsella stables; overseer and disciplinarian of young local help. Trahey, the rogue (she had nothing to base this on, but the words always went together with his name in her mind). When he was drinking, which wasn't often, she was inclined to be a little afraid of him herself. Fitz said, don't worry, he's shy of women, and anyway he's worth his weight in Niall's.

He would be busy now with Fitz and Mr. Mamood and Carrowkeel, but an excuse could be made later to summon him, show him to Upshaw.

"To get back to the main point," Upshaw said, "the money that will be wanted." Even on the brink of stating his elevated figures, he was in torture. Suppose he was only asking half, a quarter, enough? The storybook house. The warmth of fires in inclement rain, the food, the being waited upon. The ease of these unblemished comely people. From his window before tea, he had seen a swan drifting by in the water, under the wet swept droop of the willow branches. The lovely bird, the grace and sliding stillness of it, the peace and privilege it suggested, took him like a rise of burning vomit in the throat.

They and their swans. And their horses. And that Arab offering a quarter of a million pounds which they didn't want or need, obviously—

Relax. View this as a first installment.

"Ten thousand pounds," he said, and then cleared his throat. It had come out a bit uncertain and rough-edged, almost a question rather than a statement. Do it again. "Ten thousand pounds."

It wasn't hard to manage the stunned wide-eyed, "Oh, but that's *impossible!*" It came quite naturally.

"Don't tell me impossible, Mrs. Kinsella. I know people like you have funds tied up. Maybe you can't put your hand on that sum as fast as I'd whistle, but you can dip in here, dip in there, collect it up, of course you can."

The delay she had wanted now being offered her with what

could be considered ludicrous promptings of encouragement.

"Well, I don't know, it might be a matter of weeks and even then I . . ."

He cut across her. "Days, Mrs. K., not weeks at all. Would you take a week to call the fire department if this house was burning down?"

Go back to vagueness. A helpless flutter of hands. *Mrs. K.*—but ignore the sly intimacy of that. "I suppose I can get in touch with you somewhere . . ."

"I thought that was understood. Where else but right here? I've got to keep you under my eye, surely you can see that."

Should he have asked twenty thousand? Ah well, tomorrow is another day. "People like you," he went on, to clarify further, "people with money can be off at will to New York or San Francisco or Baden-Baden," which he pronounced with a long *a,* making it sound Gaelic. "Just pack a bag and flash a passport, that's all."

Stay on top now when she was down. Show himself in bold command of the situation, of details large and small. "I imagine your brother-in-law could lend me a shirt or so, he seems about my size. Maybe Mrs. Broth could pick me up some socks in the town." A change of underwear too, but he decided delicately he would save that request for Mrs. Broth's ears.

"And if those in residence want to know what your cousin from Skibbereen is doing here, just tell them the truth. That I'm waiting to receive a check—at this address—and then I'll be moving on."

Between the Arabs and the Vietnamese, what is this country coming to? Mrs. Broth inquired of herself as she left her second glass of sherry and her game of patience to admit after his thwack of the knocker Calvin Banning.

He was a tall thin man, immaculately turned out, in his late thirties, with a high balding forehead and a long face at once closed and knowing. His post was somewhat mysterious: secretary/man of affairs/majordomo in the establishment of General Loc Nou, their nearest neighbor, a quarter of a mile away.

"Where is everybody, and more specifically where is Mistress Sara?" he asked in his tenor Oxfordian voice. "I couldn't raise her in her digs."

"She's usually in the tub at this hour. As to everybody else, planting things, trading horses, talking to relatives. How is the General?"

She felt a continuing lively curiosity in the retired Vietnamese army officer. He had arrived in Leam a year ago and was reported —nobody quite able to pin down the source of this—as having brought with him two and a half tons of gold. Perhaps with some of this, he had bought Dunragh Castle and brought in squads of local men to rid it of bats, rats, and the damp malaise of abandonment. He had furnished it in French and English antiques. Banning had been very active in this, shuttling from Christie's to Sotheby Parke Bernet, dashing from Paris to London to New York. A dispenser of money and work, and a magnificent source of gossip, General Loc Nou had no trouble in becoming the uncrowned king of this quiet pocket of Connemara.

Where, Mrs. Broth often wondered, did you keep two and a half *tons* of gold? In what strongroom, what cellars? And was it in bars, or slabs the size of refrigerators?

"General Nou," Banning said, "is hale and well, almost alarmingly so. He's been riding Maravin. In the rain."

"Oh well, I suppose he's used to mud and trenches and so on," Mrs. Broth said. "Or rice paddies? They're quite wet we're told. I must get back to my labors—is there anything—?"

A door slammed distantly in the kitchen. Nobody but Trahey slammed doors.

"If you'll just see that Ms. Parry gets this." Banning gave her a heavy creamy envelope with the addressee's name written small and firm, and in the lower corner, "By hand."

He's wasting his time, the General, with Fitz on the immediate premises, Mrs. Broth thought. She attended Banning's exit and then went to see what Trahey might be up to in her kitchen.

He was leaning against the sink counter. A short square bull-chested man with a rocky red face, a wide small turned-up nose serrated at the tip, thick coarse yellow hair and yellow brows and lashes over small deeply set ice-blue eyes. His low forehead bulged out above the eyebrows. Sara said his facial conformation looked like the white clay objects in florists' windows around St. Patrick's day, Hibernian heads in the hollowed tops of which shamrocks or green grass were planted to simulate hair. His mouth was truculent and elfin, and when he smiled, which was rarely, he showed small bad teeth.

"They want whiskey," he said. "I suppose you have it under lock and key as usual?"

"What's it to you, you must have a vat of it in your own quarters," Mrs. Broth observed without any implied criticism. She and Trahey got on in a cool live-and-let-live way. "I thought Arabs didn't drink."

"This one does apparently."

After some hesitation Mrs. Broth decided on the Waterford tumblers; business was business. She took from the shelf a fresh bottle of Niall's and gave the oval silver tray an unnecessary whisk of her apron.

"The animal's bought." Trahey, a man of few words, offered no details, no price.

He wasn't a confidant of hers at any time, but Mrs. Broth felt a strong need to complain to somebody. "There's a man arrived here this morning, a gowser-looking class of fellow."

The blue eyes burned icier with sudden sharp interest. "A man? What man?"

"Have you ever heard of a cousin of theirs named Upshaw? I know *she* didn't recognize him at all when she first laid eyes on him. It seems he's to stay here a few days. But he's been put in the maid's poor room."

Trahey fingered the roll neck of his heavy dark sweater. "What's he doing here?"

"So far nothing but sleeping and stuffing himself with cake and sandwiches. Right now they're having a conference in her sitting room. Behind closed doors. She never closes her door there."

"No," he said with an inward-looking gaze. "No, I never heard of a cousin called Upshaw."

He went out, crossed the back bridge, and paused thoughtfully under a rowan tree beside a low wall. He was very much tempted to unscrew the cap and help himself to a nip, against Moira Broth's kitchen information, which had given him a peculiar blow in the ribs. But for all he knew rich men wouldn't drink from a bottle already opened, for fear of being poisoned.

The stables were on the far side of the exercise track. L-shaped, built of limestone, sturdy and graceful under immense beeches. Fitz and Mamood were standing in front of Belclare's stall.

"—now that," Fitz was saying, "is a horse of another color."

Carrowkeel was a chestnut, Belclare a silver-white. Mamood gave the breeder a puzzled look.

"Do I know her? It seems to me I remember—was the sire Clarekillen?"

"Yes. But she's half promised, we're just a bit at odds now about the price and—"

Trahey placed the refreshments on a pail of water, and Fitz, obviously about to begin on his skillful dickering, raised a dismissing thank-you hand.

Bel too heard the door slam. It seemed to provide a cue for ending an interview that was going nowhere.

She got up. "There are things I must attend to."

"Yes, all right," Upshaw said, as though in approval of domestic duties and concerns. "But one thing to clear up. I come and go as I please, do I? I don't plan to be kept under room arrest, or parked in the butler's pantry just to be out of everybody's way."

Over her shoulder, "Yes. You come and go as you please."

To illustrate his freedom, Upshaw, although not addicted to exercise, decided on a stroll about the demesne. It wouldn't hurt to get a feel of the funds involved outside as well as inside the house. For future planning.

Because he had her, he knew he had her, in his back pocket. White and ill and hardly able to speak when she saw the photograph of the two of them. Leaving out the larger matter, Kinsella's probable fiddling of the woman's will, this was a lovely bonus. What people wouldn't do, thought Upshaw, to save face. Especially women.

Except for the house island, which was tended, mown, and flowery, there was no particular plan as far as he could see to the Kinsella landscape. Hills and woods, deep soft dimples of meadow. On a grassy ridge which could be viewed from the house, a row of seven life-size Grecian ladies in flowing folds, against a great dark hedge of yew, offered some promising suggestion of grandeur. But close up, tapped by a finger, they weren't marble at all. Plaster, white, blotched and rippled with moldy green. One of them had her uplifted arm missing, nothing left but the heavy wire, with a languidly drooping hand at the top.

Almost losing his way in a grove of thick old bronze-purple monkey-puzzle trees, reminding him of Powerscourt but not planted in a kingly *allée* as there, he came upon a small stone building. Impelled by strong curiosity, he went with his natural caution from bole to bole of the beeches surrounding the cottage, and from one side, close against the stone, allowed himself a quick peek over the sprigged sash curtain.

He saw Sara Parry, flat on her back on the yellow carpet, wearing a dark brown body stocking. Eyes closed—good God, she wasn't drunk, was she? Or dead? A Siamese cat was curled near her head. As he watched, the cat yawned, the woman's eyes opened, and she swung one slender leg over the other to reach the palm of an outstretched arm. Then she swung the other leg to the other arm. He was subject to the provincial Irishman's muffling modesty and contented himself with thinking she had a nice figure, without analyzing its various components.

The hand on his shoulder took him like a thunderclap.

"What the hell do you think you're doing?" a harsh voice said in his ear.

Trahey had been following the man in the cheap blue suit for twenty minutes. Close up, he agreed with Moira Broth's poor opinion of him as far as quality went.

Upshaw returned the compliment. He didn't like the looks of Trahey at all, nor his manner of addressing him.

"I am a guest of the house," he said. "I am having a look round before dinner. I am Mrs. Kinsella's cousin."

"Cousin is it?" Trahey had no obligations beyond the stables. He saw no reason to be polite to this Peeping Tom. "The cottage happens to be a private place. I'll thank you to move along away from it."

Still unnerved from his fright—how long had this man been silently at his heels, and why?—Upshaw walked toward the drive, Trahey at his side like an escorting policeman.

In an attempt to get back his superior standing, guest, relative, Upshaw visibly and audibly sniffed. Manure.

"What luck with the horse?" he asked.

Trahey favored him with a stare. "What horse is that?"

Upshaw's face turned red with anger and insult. Fine way to treat a guest. I'll fix this bastard one way or another, by God I will, just give me a little time.

But feeling, as all near observers did, Trahey's projection of raw, ready power, he decided for the moment to hold his tongue. Wave the fellow off.

"Thank you, I know my way from here." Get back to your manure piles, my man.

Cousin? Trahey asked himself. *Kinsella* cousin? *Mahon* cousin? It would be wise in every way to keep an eye on this gowser until he showed a clean pair of heels.

Six

"Kiss Sara for me," Jerome Niall said in amiable innocence, bidding Conor good-bye. "And hug Bel. Safe home. My love to all concerned."

The day in Dublin had turned into a busy and festive two. He had stayed at Jerome's large house on Merrion Square, or rather snatched occasional sleep there. Friends to catch up with, a late party in Dame Street, favorite pubs where he tried to avoid the glasses served up on the house to the returning prodigal. After his school-vacation days he had managed at least every other year a week or two in this second land of his.

Telefis Eirann said yes indeed, a camera crew at any time, or well, almost, just let them know a day or so in advance.

Between one thing and another, it was after six when at the curb he disentangled himself from four beautiful blond Niall children, all under twelve. Oh well, Ireland was the only underpopulated country he knew of; Jerome had plenty of room for his charming progeny.

His waiting car was an old but reliable Morris Minor convertible. "Take it, take it," Jerome ordered. "We have three more eating their heads off in the garage."

Releasing the hand brake, he reminded Jerome, "Not a word to anyone. This is to be a surprise."

Surprise was a word to think about in another context while he was driving west across Ireland, the distance to be covered to Leam about one hundred and fifty miles. He gathered that no one here knew about the alliance between him and Sara. At the time she had said, "A little discretion, Conor, a private matter—I don't think my father would quite approve. Or more accurately, it would make him unhappy."

Her widowed father, Thomas Parry, a New Yorker by birth,

was then head of the English department at Duke University in Durham, North Carolina, and there was very little crossing of paths to worry about.

He wondered if she had told Bel and Fitz, and then decided she probably hadn't. It did not go with Sara's nature—having ended an affair or having it ended for her, depending on how you looked at it—to dither on about the dear old days when she and Conor had lived in love.

And she was hardly a breast-beater or utterer of "Mea culpa's." Perhaps fifty years ago, a Sara Parry might have said to a man who was thinking of marrying her, "There's something you must know about me, Fitz."

No, not even fifty years back. Sara was too civilized. She would have known even then what secrets to keep.

We would have married, Conor thought. Of course we would have married. We just didn't get around to it. Before her films, before NBC. Before "Take your hands off my girl" and "One way or another you wouldn't be there, would you."

Maynooth, Edenderry, Tullamore. He knew the road well. He had driven or been driven along it a great many times since the summer when he was ten. His mother, Ivy, had run away with a friend of his father's, and after a great many trans-Atlantic telephone calls and cables Conor was dispatched to Leam to stay with his Aunt Bel and Uncle Paul.

The rent in the marriage was repaired. Ivy came home in September. But many a following summer Conor went back to Leam. "It's cheaper than camp," said Ivy, conveniently overlooking the round-trip air fare. "And he is fond of his cousins. Such a nice country life for a city boy."

Paul Kinsella usually took off the months of July and August, and had been a loved second father; especially as his own father, an archeologist, was away from home in New York at least six months of every year.

This is a dirty trick on Fitz, he told himself severely as he pulled up in front of a familiar little pub in Horseleap just a half mile away from Moate. But then a sharp cold reconsideration: *What* is a dirty trick on Fitz?

This might be a completely hopeless mission.

Fitz, four years alone, was probably more than ready for marriage. He was not in any sense a bachelor by nature. But would Sara, New York and Hollywood and Paris and London Sara, want to bury herself in Leam?

Hardly burial. Fitz said the income from his chosen work meant either a feast or a famine. There were the feasts, though, and he was fond of Paris and liked an occasional business-with-pleasure jaunt to New York.

Hardly burial, in any case, if he had moved into the center of her world.

Have another drink and dismiss the idea that she was already signed and sealed and had delivered herself with love to Paul Fitzacre Kinsella.

His entrance lines were already written—simple, natural. He was looking for a rest and change, he wanted to see Bel and Fitz, too bad Monica is in Iraq, and oh, isn't it nice that Sara Parry is here too.

But why didn't you write, dear? I wanted to surprise you, Bel. And I am on assignment here although there's no great rush about it.

Mrs. Meany, behind the bar, studied him with interest. A remarkable looking class of man, she thought. Alone but not lonely, somehow at ease with himself. Supple strong body, suit of fine thin gray tweed. Strong face, but like an ode—now where did *that* word spring from, she asked herself. Anyway, a harking-back kind of face, generations forcefully presenting themselves in the brow, the long aquiline nose and shapely mouth.

Is it that I've seen him before or is this just for the pleasure of looking at him?

He felt her gaze and lifted his eyes, gray or blue, she wasn't sure, deep-set and clear. Behind her porcelain beer pump handle painted with roses, she blushed, and was saved by a flicker of memory.

She smiled at him as he came over to the bar. "Sorry to stare you out of house and home. But I remember now. Sixteen, you were, your face and head all blood when they brought you in here. You took your brandy like a man. An automobile accident, wasn't it?"

He hadn't forgotten the accident, but he had failed to connect it with this smoky little pub. Fitz was driving, showing off, going much too fast down a hill and around a tight curve. They came upon a donkey and cart mysteriously straddling the road—turning around perhaps?—and Fitz jammed on the brakes, missed the donkey and the driver but smashed into the rear of the cart. Conor in the open car was thrown into the air and then face down into the remains of the cart.

Later, he had wondered about it. In a natural way for their age, he and Fitz were occasional rivals. There had been a girl, a red-haired girl, he'd just taken from Fitz . . .

He smiled back at Mrs. Meany. "Brandy, and then you let me lie down blood and all and put a blanket over me—yes, right over there opposite where I'm sitting now, and called the doctor."

"Who said just flesh wounds, and you'd live to fight another day. In honor of your survival, will you drink with me?"

Warmed, he clinked glasses with her and thought that although it was not exactly his country, it was nice to be back, remembered, greeted, and toasted in the house's very best scotch.

He stayed for a salmon sandwich which, in this remote little place was nevertheless served on his favorite brown bread with fresh lemon, capers, and a faint dusting of cayenne. Hot coffee and a short brandy—he detested the concoction known as Irish coffee—and then off again, the rain now apparently having decided to declare itself a permanent fixture for the night.

Time to pick up his heels; he didn't want his arrival to rock a sleeping household. There was no way of bypassing the city of Galway, perched between Lough Corrib and the Bay. This slowed him, but then he picked up speed again. It was a little after nine-thirty when he stopped the car and lifted the heavy latch of the strong but airy, high wrought-iron gate between its grass-grown walls of stone.

Rain rushing through the trees to the right and left made waterfall noises. As he was putting his car in the garage on the near side of the house pond, he was startled by a mighty leaping surge and barking. Switching on the garage light he said, "If it isn't Vesper," and was joyously embraced, paws on his shoulders.

Vesper, the wolfhound, tremendous, almost pony-size, a dog of unquestioned authority, but kind and gentle to his own and with an excellent memory for that occasional member of his family,

Conor Niall. "But if I'd been a horse thief, Vesper, God help me," Conor told him with a caress of the great rough-haired head.

He was escorted across the bridge, and Vesper in a mannerly fashion ignored the kitchen entrance and led him under dripping willows around the curve of the house to the front.

Turning, at the door, he looked across the water to light just faintly visible through the beeches, in the cottage. It would be nice after all this time and all these miles to go straight there, and say, "Sara," and hear her say his name.

"I think she and Fitz might make a pair." What if they were making a pair right now? There was no one to see the wave of deep red that heated the skin of his face.

Vesper, puzzled, nudged his knee. Like most dogs and cats, he was nervous of someone standing unaccountably still.

He raised the brass-ring knocker and let it fall with one good resounding thump. There were lights in the french windows on either side, veiled for the night in long folds of pale silk ninon.

Silence. But then, if Mrs. Broth still wore her high-laced sneakers he wouldn't hear her feet on the marble. Suddenly, no doubt while pelting down the stairs, an unmistakable poodle bark: Peach.

The door opened. There was the confusion of Peach trying to get out to greet the visitor, the larger Vesper seeking to get in past this obstacle, and the fact that a total stranger stood just inside with the knob in his hand.

A sallow-skinned underfed-looking man in a wrinkled blue suit.

"I'm not a servant, you know," he said, "but who was it you're after wanting?"

"Everybody," Conor said, and identified himself.

"Well, come in then. I'm a cousin too. Distant though. John Upshaw. From Skibbereen." Still with his air of slight proprietary suspicion, he studied the English trench coat, the dancing welcoming Peach, the well-traveled suitcase placed in the center of the hall by a confident hand.

Conor thought later he should have been warned then, but he wasn't. Apart from a mild and fleeting curiosity—a *cousin?*—the man at that time barely touched his notice. People did drop in on Bel, all kinds of people. This had always been a hospitable house.

"Now, as to everybody. Bel," the syllable sounding strange on his tongue, tentative, "went up early, said she was tired. James," and again the almost apologetic use of the given name, "is I don't know where. He's gone out. His greenhouse, maybe. He spends a lot of time in it. Fitz is at the cottage with Sara—he seems to like it there." Was there an invisible wink in the lift of the man's odd sibilant voice? "Mrs. Broth went to Galway to see a film."

It was Upshaw's second day in the house. And the first time, behind their backs, he had allowed himself to use first names.

Thinking about the bedroom that was usually his, Conor picked up his bag. "Is there anyone else staying here besides you?"

"Not at the moment, and I have a skinflint bit of a back room you wouldn't mind being put out of." He drew for this aggrieved statement a mystified look.

"You have quite a grasp on the human topography here. I'll see myself upstairs." The large room, next to Fitz's, was empty of an occupant but not of comfort. French wallpaper panels, depicting deep misty woods at dawn, all around it, fire laid ready, swelling bronze silk-covered down puff on the big bamboo-patterned brass bed. Rain against the panes emphasized the ease and solidity within.

An ill-disposed observer might have criticized the soft float of dust balls in a corner, the marks of muddy paws on the faded green carpet, and the water stain on the ceiling over the door—the loose crescent shape of the Windward Islands, gazed at, cherished, in childhood—but to him they conveyed the peace of an old, well-used, experienced house.

It was pleasant to see left-behind paperbacks of his in the bookshelves between two of the windows, and find an old raincoat in the ceiling-high wardrobe. To discover while hastily unpacking a forgotten clean folded handkerchief monogrammed C.N. in the top left-hand dresser drawer. He had not been tidied away, then. The room had been waiting for him.

Bag empty and stowed in the wardrobe, he went to the window nearest him. It overlooked the stone cottage—not at the moment, with its two occupants, appealing to dwell upon. He thought that at some time he would probably hear Fitz returning to his bedroom, if and when he did. Like a goddamned housemother—with a sharp impatient turn from the window.

If Bel had gone up early and tired, better not burst in on her.

He had no desire to engage in a downstairs conversation with the cousin Upshaw, who might wish to offer tales of an ailing mother or an uncle's prize bull; although he had no look, come to think of it, of the country about him. More that of the city and its meaner streets. In which case, he might want the loan of some money from yet another new-found relative.

James offered an ideal opportunity. Wandering about looking for James to say hello to would present no air of snooping. First a drink and then the stroll.

He was a little bothered by this hair-splitting scheming and decided to drop it then and there. He hadn't all the time in the world, but just a little over two weeks to take care of the business he'd come on.

Tiptoeing was out.

Now what in God's name is this? Upshaw asked himself, returning to the library fire but unable to sit down.

I arrive here only yesterday and here the very next day is a man come all the way from the United States of America. If his coming wasn't a secret, why wouldn't they have talked about it? Surely they'd be excited to see someone from so far off.

Hold still now. Look before you leap. If she had summoned her nephew—big formidable-looking fellow he was at that—could he have made it this fast? Yes. Get on a plane in New York at night, arrive in the early morning in Shannon, on to Dublin, and then get cracking to Leam.

But there hadn't been any open suspicion or, goadingly, even any interest in that first glance in the hall. Which meant exactly nothing. He might be a deep one.

Or maybe like these people he just came and went at his pleasure, a journey over the Atlantic as casual a thing to him as town-to-town on a bus to those more hampered in the way of funds and leisure.

Face up to the man. Feel him out. If he started to get cold feet now, he'd have lost the game which he had begun so well by looking like winning, all the cards in his hand.

If everything tumbles to pieces, I can always cut and run. Say I never said a word to her. It's all her guilty imagination. All I did was tell her how much I admired her late husband the first and only time I met him.

Conor was running down the stairs with his trench coat over his shoulder when his way at the bottom was all but barred by Upshaw.

Anxious voice, words speeded up. "It's a shame to show so little interest. You all the way from the States and nobody here to greet you—I thought I'd do my bit to make up for it. Will you have a drink with me? The library fire's doing well."

It was only his natural courtesy which persuaded Conor to take the time for the one drink.

In the library, Upshaw went to the well-stocked tray on the great dark teak writing desk inlaid with mother-of-pearl. What an insinuating way of moving he has, Conor thought, as if he was used to slipping silently through half-closed doors. While a native of an overtly democratic nation, he concluded that there had been an unfortunate marriage somewhere within the circle of his relatives and that Upshaw was the product of it.

"Will you take a drop of the family potion?" Upshaw held up a bottle of Niall's. "If I say so myself, it's a good drink."

"Yes, all right. No ice." To emphasize the fact that this was to be a brief interval, he half sat on the arm of a leather chair.

Upshaw gave him his drink and with his own sat down in the chair on the other side of the hearth. "*Slainte.* Now let's see— you're the lawyer, was it?"

"No."

"Or did I hear doctor?"

No help for it; satisfy his curiosity and get it over with. Conor gave him a two-sentence description of his profession. A little amused by having in effect to produce his credentials in this second home of his, and to a stranger who looked as if he didn't belong there, he added, "You sound a bit like a detective. Placing members of the household so accurately on the map. And now— lawyer, doctor is it?—checking my references." He half smiled into his drink. "Has someone here committed a crime I haven't heard about?"

A dull color came up under the sallow skin. "I did not mean to offend," Upshaw said in a winded way. "I only wanted to show interest."

Seven

Hail the conquering hero comes. Under, Conor qualified, his big black umbrella.

James's greenhouse lay to the far left on the other side of the bridge. He saw it lit and decided that James among his flowers and greens would not feel himself deprived if saying hello to him was deferred for a bit.

He had, not particularly by choice, Vesper beside him. He foresaw an ungraceful arrival, the two of them, Vesper hugely shaking water all over Sara's little room.

No flashlight was needed; the lighted house windows reflected in water sent up a gentle illumination which turned the rain to a driving flight of diamonds.

He was in the center of the thirty-foot bridge when through the sound of rain-tossed trees, and from far away, came a faint ragged kind of cry. He stopped and Vesper stopped too, tense against his leg. A bird perhaps, or a little animal pounced upon. Or a drunken voice lifted, someone trudging along the road to the west of the demesne, on his wavering way home from McCane's bar.

Vesper, superbly trained, did not move a muscle but looked up at him with large imploring amber eyes. "Okay, Vesper," he said, "a run in the woods won't hurt you. You know your way home."

The dog swept the remaining length of the bridge and disappeared. Conor under his umbrella walked steadily on, his measured pace reminding him of a British bobby about to arrive on the scene and ask the classic question, "Now then, what's going on here?"

Ducking under dripping branches, he stopped at the door of the stone cottage and gave it a crisp double knock.

The walls were too thick to emit readable sounds from within, but he sensed in his blood silence, then words, then movement. He had put down his umbrella. There was no sheltering roof over the doorstep and rain found its way down the back of his neck.

To his left the cottage extended in an ell where an extra bedroom had been added. The lights in it went suddenly and inhospitably out.

How long could a minute or so last?

Hail, the conquering zero comes.

Who *is* that nuisance at the door? No, thank you, we do not want the Encyclopaedia Britannica. Our vacuum cleaner is in perfect working order, thank you.

It was a horrible thought that he might have an expression on his face as affronted as that of Upshaw's. "I only wanted to show interest."

The door opened. Light poured out, and music, turned low. Fitz said, "Well, in the name of the Father, Son, Holy Ghost, and NBC!" and then in a voice turned down like the radio, "Come in for God's sake."

Take off his coat or not? He went so far as to undo the belt. "Why the whisper?" he asked in his normal vibrating voice.

"I've just put Sara to bed. She picked up an awful chill somewhere, teeth chattering, a bit of a fever I suspect—"

Put her to bed? Undressed her, lifted her, covered her, kissed her?

But probably not. He was almost sure she was hiding, in the bedroom. A grown woman! Of all the childish dirty tricks—but however you looked at it a frightful resounding slap across the face.

Well, take a few minutes and make everybody here as uncomfortable as possible.

"I'll just go in and say good night."

"No, no. Don't wake her."

Wake her, when the bedroom light had gone off a matter of two minutes or so ago?

Sara listened in the bedroom. He echoed and re-echoed back from all her private walls.

"Coward, ass, fool," she said to herself. "But no, not with no warning. It's too much right now. I can't."

Conor found her, hiding from him as she might be, all over the room. Moving restlessly, he passed in and out of a vague pocket of her perfume near the end of the sofa. Two crushed cushions side by side. Her reading glasses on a book face down on the sofa arm, André Maurois' *Disraeli*. A slipper lost in her flight, Cinderella style; a slipper well remembered, green silk embroidered in blue. Her little silver pitcher of lilies of the valley on the lamp table. She liked as she read to pick them up and breathe them, as another would sip and savor brandy.

"Do you suppose the sound of a drink being poured out would disturb the patient?"

"Can't you lower your voice?" Fitz demanded. "You're not on the air." And then hearing himself he added, "Sorry to sound so unwelcoming. I'm delighted to see you. What brings you here, not that you need a reason?"

Conor was following him into the kitchen. At least, he thought, he's got all his clothes on, and doesn't look caught in the middle of visibly steaming passion. Fitz's hair and face were in perfect order too. No collected rose of lipstick, no distracted dreaming gaze.

Fitz poured drinks, very much the master of the house. It wasn't his yet but no doubt would be—the property had been left outright and with no strings to Bel.

He explained his presence in a somewhat slanted way. Was he protecting Sara? And if so, why? "I have an assignment to do over here, a sudden one, and I thought I'd come and see how everybody is while I'm waiting around for a camera crew. A kind of vacation."

"Welcome times three," Fitz said, lifting his glass to his cousin. "Have you eaten? There's a cold chicken pie that could be heated, and cheese—"

He had no desire at this moment to make himself at home and eat Sara's food while she was pointedly telling him to go to hell.

"No thanks, I'll swallow this and be off. Who's that man Upshaw?"

"All I know," Fitz said, applying himself to his drink with relish, "is that he's some kind of step-relative, and he's on his uppers, waiting here until he gets a check from somewhere or other to allow him to proceed on his way. And that I'm to shut up about the sale of a horse yesterday, probably two horses by tomorrow. I can only gather he might be tempted to ask for a loan on the strength of it."

The kitchen was as full of Sara as the little high-windowed sitting room. A long yellow-and-white-striped silk scarf trailing from the back of a chair, a pot of rose geranium on the windowsill scenting the air. White pigskin gloves tossed on the table suggesting, as well-worn gloves do, the shape of the hands, the bend of the fingers.

Go ahead and suffer, Sara. Hold your breath. Strain your ears. Listen with all your might and main to what I could be telling Fitz about us.

He could have blown her wide open, probably wrecked her with Fitz. It was incredibly tempting.

("Oh, while I think of it, will you give her this earring? I wanted to remember to return it to her."

"Earring? What on earth—?"

"She dropped it somewhere between the bed and the bathroom, I'm not sure but I think it's a sapphire . . ."

"What bed? What bathroom? Where? How did *you* come across it?"

"Well now, since you ask—")

Fitz was giving him a pondering look. "About your wanting to go in and say good night—did you know her in New York then? That well, I mean."

"Yes, I knew her in New York, a little."

A narrow flagged passageway led into the kitchen. From beyond it, at the front door, came a sound of nails scratching on wood and then a deep commanding, urgent bark.

"I suppose next a brass band," Fitz said, busily maintaining the fiction of a sleeping Sara. He went and opened the door and Vesper plunged in. When he shook himself, some of the spatters on the creamy linen slipcover of the chair closest to him were pink.

They both bent to the dog, who was panting and signaling softly deep in his throat. His muzzle was smeared with red: fresh blood. Conor remembered the cry he had heard on the bridge.

Fingers exploring, Fitz said, "He's not cut. He's found something and now we are requested to go and see it with him. Thanks but no thanks, Vesper."

Disturbed, Conor asked, "Suppose he's found something human? Bleeding? Dead?"

"There speaks the hungry news man. Nothing ever happens around here. People don't shoot or knife people."

"I didn't hear a shot when he bolted off, just a shout or cry."

"Are you prepared to go blinding off through the woods in the rain to investigate? Probably the rooks got an owl, they make an awful complaint, the owls, and who'd blame them?" Fitz's mild amusement at this good-deed Boy Scouting was galling but effective.

"No."

Vesper, however, could not be stilled and went whining to the door, head turned back over his shoulder to them.

"Oh hell, he'll keep this up all night, I'll go and rouse out Trahey and tell him to take a look round." Fitz got his raincoat out of a closet near the door.

And how many other garments do you keep here for your convenience, Fitz?

"Are you sure it's wise to leave the invalid alone?"

Fitz at his tone gave him a puzzled look and then smiled faintly. "She's deep in the arms of aspirin and a hot toddy. All she wants is peace and quiet."

"Ten thousand pounds."

Bel had carried the figure about with her all day and now waked to it from early, escaping sleep.

Sooner or later it would have to be, "Yes, you'll have it" or "No, you won't."

Her new-found cousin from the south might be patient, blessing them with his dubious company, for a week at most; after that there was a black blank.

In the early afternoon, walking shrinkingly around the edge of the matter and avoiding its storm center, she had forced herself to do something she knew might be unwise: call her old friend Kate Tierne, in Dublin.

"If the heirs she knocked out of her will ever found out the circumstances, there'd be the mother and father of a court fight."

They exchanged pleasantries and gossip. Gerald, Kate said, was in Brussels helping to rewrite international law, something to do with copyrights or patents, she wasn't sure which.

"Oh, by the way, just to settle a little argument that Fitz and I had—he's so much better about figures than I am—can you recall or did you ever hear what sum it was that Amy Veagh left to us?" She was alarmed to find that she was shaking. Not just her hand holding the receiver; shaking all over.

What a ridiculous question. Would Kate think it so? And over tea tables say, "Bel Kinsella asked me the strangest thing . . ."

"Oh lord, you know my memory. All that comes to mind is that it was sort of a lot, or seemed so at the time."

"How much in your financial view is sort of a lot?"

Pinned down, Kate said promptly, "Anything over twenty thousand pounds. But Fitz is in and out of Dublin, he can look up the will any time he likes."

"Yes, of course." Hastily, Bel switched to James's lemon lilies, just out this morning. And was it as cold in Dublin as it was in Leam? See you soon, Kate dear.

Now, listening to the rain, she moved her head restlessly on the pillow. Fitz, would you mind looking up Amy Veagh's will? Why, Mother?

Or, Fitz, a dear friend—I won't say who because that would be giving things away—in any case, she must have ten thousand pounds within the week. I'm sure she'll pay it back— But it wouldn't be paid back even if Fitz went along with this wild request, which was highly unlikely.

She had considered and reconsidered that time-honored emergency measure of the troubled: go to her priest, who would be bound in secrecy. But what could kind old Father Fenn do about any of it? And would it be tantamount to confessing for Paul an ugly last sin and asking in effect for posthumous absolution?

What, in her place, would a woman of courage and daring, of cool intellect do?

Command John Upshaw to leave the house immediately and devil take the hindmost. Who was the hindmost, she or Paul?

Let Amy Veagh's heirs go ahead and sue, and if they collected—perhaps with heavy damages—all right, they collected.

A woman with any intellect at all—just to be on the safe side in case she changed her powerful mind—would certainly try to find out from Fitz exactly what the Kinsella financial position was. Do that tomorrow.

Facing up to things wouldn't be too awful for her, not really, when the story came out. When she had lost Paul she knew she had lost pretty well everything.

It wouldn't be nice for Fitz, but he was young and strong and confident, doing what he wanted to do and doing it well; and with luck there would be Sara to turn to for comfort.

The only one it would be really terrible for was Paul.

Because he couldn't answer. He couldn't deny or erase this published last chapter of his life. A secret amorous meeting with a doomed woman, its purpose triumphantly accomplished. Her will changed at the last minute, her money switched to his greedy outstretched hands.

Her bold hypothetical woman vanished into mist. This creature too was trapped and helpless.

Not wanting to risk a hail from beyond the half-open library door, Conor went quickly and quietly past it, crossed the unlighted indigo-walled dining room and pushed open the swinging door to the butler's pantry. Hunger was asserting itself in spite of his preoccupation with rage.

How are you going to explain to Fitz, Sara, that you couldn't bear me face to face? You have to know someone reasonably well to dislike an encounter so much that you hide behind a door, trampling all over your own dignity. But you may think it will all blow away, you may be laboring under the happy delusion that I'm just here overnight and will be off and gone tomorrow.

James was sitting at the kitchen table eating crackers and sipping milk. He jumped to his feet. "My dear, *dear* Conor!" and then he blushed at this openly expressed surprised delight. "When did you get here? I slipped in the back way just now because . . ."

He hesitated and Conor said, "Yes, I know. Library possibly occupied." He hugged James; you were allowed to do this in Ireland. "Where is your family feeling? A new cousin to be taken to your bosom."

"I did my stint this morning," James said. "Have some crackers? I showed him over the greenhouse and the gardens. I must say he doesn't seem to know a tearose from a tea towel. Or cold roast beef? As I remember you like cold roast beef. Beer too. I'd join you except—" He patted his midriff.

Conor, answering his eager questions on the life of a television journalist, fixed himself a plate of beef with Mrs. Broth's curried cucumber pickle ("Pickle at this hour? Curry?" James wondered. "You must be ironclad inside.") and soda bread and butter. He was consuming it, with a pint mug of Harp beer, when the kitchen door was opened.

Trahey, his black plastic coat dripping and glistening, his yellow hair flattened on his forehead, demanded, "Where's Fitz?"

"At the cottage probably. Did you find anything?"

"Yes," Trahey said. "A lad, Gorman—I knew him *not* to say hello to— Dead, drowned in the stream across the road and west of the back gate. It's a bad spot, particularly when you've been raising a glass at McCane's. He's on the bank now, safe and dry so to speak, Vesper's standing watch. Will one of you call the Garda or will I?"

The place where the young man had met his death was on Kinsella property and was therefore in a fringe way Kinsella responsibility. But it was a matter of often-repeated popular trespass. If you were walking east after leaving the town, you could cut off a good quarter mile by leaving the road and taking to the footpath across Kinsella land with its amiably low accessible walls and fences.

Near the road, the path crossed a narrow hurtling stream with steep banks, jaggedly rocky. Two planks, unrailed, went from bank to bank. A balancing act easy enough by day but treacherous in the wet and windy night, with rowan branches whipping at the balancer.

The sadly simple explanation arrived at and offered by the two young Gardai—gratefully drinking tots of whiskey poured by Fitz, in the kitchen—was that Aloysius Gorman ("the poor soul's friends such as they were called him 'Wishy'") had had a few, fallen off the planks, hit his head on one of the harshly pointed rocks, and rolled unconscious into the stream. Of course, there would be a post mortem, but that looked to be about the lay of it.

"I knew him," Fitz interrupted. "He worked here for a while. Poor kid, ranting witch of an old mother trying to beat religion into him with a stick, wanting him to be a priest, but I don't think he had the wits for it."

The Garda Sergeant Grady said almost hopefully, "Of course, it may not be as simple as it looks. He could have been pushed I suppose, although why is beyond me. But it would be an easy way to douse a man for good, no weapons required. I can't think off-hand of any likely murderers in our midst. You wouldn't"--looking at Fitz--"have seen any strangers about here lately?"

Fitz and Conor and James were sitting at the round table with the Gardai. Upshaw was standing just outside the doorway.

He had been undressing for bed, thinking he'd had by now enough whiskey. It wouldn't do to go too deeply into the drink while there was an important and tricky business matter on hand.

The sound of the sirens through the rain pierced him, stopped him dead in his shirt, socks, and underpants. He pulled his trousers back on and buckled his belt with shaking hands.

Well, he had his story ready. She made it all up, sir, every word of it. The story didn't sound so good now.

He listened for a while at the top of the stairs, and heard from a doorwayed distance men's voices in what might be the kitchen. He was suddenly reminded of his own weight, one hundred and fifty-two pounds. A cold draft of air from somewhere set him shivering.

Were the sirens just a passing terror, Garda on their way somewhere else?

Escape from the house right now would be easy, windows all around. He had two pounds and a little change in his pocket, enough for buses heading home.

But slipping off like that would proclaim and prove his guilt. From then on, a hunted man.

Unable to resist the burning necessity to find out, to know what was to be coped with or what his fate was to be, he crept inch by inch, foot by foot, to the butler's pantry, where he flattened himself against the wall in near-darkness.

Garda coming in now, two of them from the sound of it--

And then it turned out to be all, Jesus, right. Never say die. Somebody else's trouble.

After hearing what it was all about, he allowed himself to be seen and heard. "Did I hear a siren? Is something wrong?"

"A sad accident, a drowning," James said. "Sorry to interrupt, sergeant."

"Strangers?" Fitz said. "Only my cousin here, Mr.—John is it?— Upshaw, and he looks to be quite dry . . ."

"Oh, I didn't mean that kind of stranger. How do you do, Mr. Upshaw. We're off now. Yes, sad thing, sad. Although not to put too fine a point upon it, he wasn't good for much, poor Gorman."

"Nice little memorial statement," Conor said ten minutes later to Fitz as the two went up the stairs.

Outside his bedroom door, Fitz yawned. "I suppose—pursuing as you were whichever of us you were so eager to see, in the cottage—you'll feel unhappy about not going after that cry you heard. If you'd reacted sooner . . . a life being ended. Horrible, isn't it?"

Conor felt as though a bruised foot had been purposely, heavily stamped upon. *"Probably the rooks got an owl."*

"I'd been thinking the same thing. But," voice hard, "I've gotten to the place where I find life too short for if-only."

Eight

It was one of those nights when you felt you hadn't slept more than an hour or so while actually you had garnered five or six hours of intermittent unconsciousness. The waking, tossing time seeming so long, the in-between slumber brief and dream-ridden.

Sara so near, but placing herself so far away. One thing Conor supposed he was listening for was the sound of a car, leaving, no matter how late the hour.

"I'll just be off, Fitz, to"—some little inn, some secret town—"and let me know when he's gone, will you?"

At a little after two he gave up for a while, turned on the lamp and picked up his book. A barely audible knock on his door brought him upright with a heavily pounding heart. "I am so sorry, Conor, about hiding. I just came to say a proper good night to you."

He went to the door and found Bel standing outside, wrapped in a pale blue wool robe.

"I am so sorry," Bel whispered, "to disturb you at this hour I mean."

He put an arm about her and drew her into the room.

He gave her a hearty kiss. "I didn't want to wake *you,* earlier. I'm so happy to see you, Bel."

Violet eyes very wide, she said, "I thought I was dreaming. I was half asleep, oh, hours ago, and I thought I heard your voice, you and Fitz, and it seemed too good to be true. Then I went to get another pill and saw the little crack of light. Darling Conor, how absolutely wonderful."

Talk about a welcome from the heart, he thought. Bel very nearly made up for the stunning rejection not far back.

"Can I give you a drink, Bel, from your, my, twenty-first birthday flask? Better for you than a pill."

"No, I just wanted to see if my ears were deceiving me, and now if my eyes are."

Something about the eyes, always large and now larger, made him ask abruptly, "Is everything all right?"

"Everything is lovely now that you're here."

He had been wondering whether to tell her about the death of the young man, on her property, in her stream, and this decided him to let it wait until morning. "Good night, darling," her hand lightly stroking his cheek. She turned away fast but not before he saw the sparkle of tears under her eyes. The tears raised a question in his mind. No doubt gratifying if you didn't know your aunt so well, but oddly unlike her; she wasn't an easy weeper. From behind, in her swift departing move to the door and out, she looked a little bent into herself. Bel didn't bend, she was pliantly straight as a willow.

He thought about it for ten minutes before sleep unexpectedly swallowed him again.

A mental alarm clock woke him at six. If Sara hadn't left in the dead of night, she might very well do so early in the morning.

Behind a closed door in the bathroom on the other side of Fitz's room, water was running into the tub. Not desiring to interrupt Upshaw in his possible ablutions in the maid's bath on the third floor, he took the only alternative.

On a half-landing on the stairway going down to the deep cool stone cellars was a narrow room that held the usual bathroom equipment as well as a dusty Exercycle, gymnast's rings dangling by ropes from hooks in the ceiling, a trapeze, a punching bag, and a collection of jump ropes slung over a nail. One of the Mahon boys—Luke was it?—had been a devoted body builder.

In twelve minutes, showered and shaved, he was out and running up the stone steps into the big silent empty kitchen. Mrs. Broth had long done away with early-morning tea trays. "Those who wish their cup at that hour might like to think of putting a hot plate in their rooms." Coffee was too much trouble and took too much time; he ate a fast bread-and-butter sandwich and drank a cup of strong tea.

Sara was an early riser, or had been. She said her head was freshest for work then. Looking inspectingly down at himself—fawn corduroy pants, brown-and-white striped shirt, yellow Shetland pullover she'd given him—he went out the kitchen door into the soft June morning, the sun drawing mists from cold soaked earth and trees and grass. Puffs and swirls and eddies of white and smoky silver moving, swaying in a light breeze. Like walking, he thought, through a ballet set. All that was missing was the music.

No answer to his knock at the door of the cottage. He went around to the kitchen end and looked through the window. Empty coffee cup, plate with a few toast crumbs on it, sitting in the sink.

Again, my bird has flown.

But the gloves were still there, and the scarf. She couldn't be with Fitz, he was in the bathtub or just freshly out of it; Fitz was a great soaker in the mornings. A peculiar stirring on his skin surface told him he sensed her not far away.

If she was being evasive again, she would probably be in the woods, not wandering openly on the grassy dips and rises. There was a promising stretch of hilly woodland just beyond the beech coppice. It was sweet now with the songs of thrush and robin. And there it is after all, the ballet music.

Feeling in some way lost in time, he went very quietly through birches and then into the scented gloom of tremendous old pines. His throat was tight with the effort of not, jubilantly, shouting her name, sending it ringing through the trees.

He saw her before she saw him. Sunlight through the high branches finding and losing her, but she was a lighted-looking girl at any and all hours. A kind of built-in responsive awareness, gaiety in her tilted eyes and lifting mouth corners, a very fair radiance of hair and skin, an appearance of having been newly minted, just this moment.

She was perhaps forty feet away from him and the reason her eyes hadn't gone in his direction, her water-green eyes, was that she was intent on something just ahead of her, unseen by him.

"Cairin!" she cried. The Siamese trotted to her with a helpless wild flutter of blue in her mouth. "Cairin, you *dreadful—*" She bent and seized the cat's back with one hand, prying open its jaws with the other. She stood up, holding the bird, face in distress now. She touched its back with a tentative finger and then very carefully placed it on a broad low limb. She watched it with all her soul, standing utterly still. And Conor watched her with all his. The short straight nose, the charming Parry mouth, expressive and tender, relaying messages when absolutely in repose.

There was a movement of wings. And then the bird flew up into the higher branches and away. Cairin's eyes too followed its flight. Philosophically, she licked a bloodied paw.

"Sara."

At his voice, her head slowly swiveled. She wants to turn and run, he thought, he knew; but she won't. She began moving, small and slender and straight-backed, very swiftly toward him. Go ahead, say hello to Conor, and get out of this woodland trap.

There was a low leafy branch of rowan between them. She pulled it back to pass through. "Conor, how nice." Her face was a blaze of pink. She let the branch slip from her hand and it whipped him about the face and head, drawing blood at one temple. Having administered its lashing, the branch swayed softly back into place.

"The land of a thousand welcomes," Conor said, reaching into his back pocket for a handkerchief.

"I'm sorry. I don't think I know exactly what I was doing."

"Your hand knew," he said. "Here, I'd better let you through if we're to escape any more bloodshed. I'm glad, about that bird."

She stood a foot away from him, arms at her sides. Throwaway-dramatic clothes as always, a gallantly cut short cape of loden cloth, narrow flame-red pants. A leaf was caught in her hair just over the brow. "How long have you been watching, here?"

"Three, four minutes, or forever, depending on how you keep time."

He put his hands on her shoulders and studied her face, close. The wood seemed to have fallen silent and then there was a shower of song overhead and from a distance the soft rhythmic thud of hooves on the exercise track, a kind of drumbeat he felt in his blood as well as in his ears.

"My once and future Sara," he said. Their eyes locked. The words, which came out without his first thinking about them, seemed to drift up and float in the leaves above them.

"Yes, and my hail-and-farewell Conor."

"You're a little ahead of yourself." He saw something like a flash of pain and loss deep in her eyes and added in his confusion, "I gather you've recovered from your chills and fever?"

"I'm perfectly well this morning." Her voice, unlike her eyes, was calm.

"Good. It's nice to have you in fighting trim." Before she could do anything about it he put his arms around her and kissed her hard, greeting her in no uncertain terms with all of his body. She was docile for a moment, soft; she drank from his well.

Or. Was she just apologizing, getting this over with? As though in answer she wrenched her head aside and he said firmly against her throat under her ear, "Be quiet, Sara darling, I have a lot of catching up to do."

Freeing her mouth again, she said brightly, sociably, over his shoulder, "Good morning, Calvin."

"I was wondering," the tenor voice said, "whether it might be proper to come to your assistance, or not."

"No, just an old friend I haven't seen for a time. Conor Niall, Calvin Banning."

The sunlight glistened on the high dome of Banning's forehead. His expression was amused and superior, that of a man above amorous skirmishes in the woods. His suit of bronzed green Harris tweed looked fresh from the needle of his tailor.

"Calvin," Sara explained, her voice now unsteady and her face still a stinging delicate pink, "is—what?—the cornerstone of General Nou's establishment. Dunragh Castle."

"Actually, I wasn't snooping," Banning said. "I heard there had been trouble here, a young man dead, and was taking a shortcut to the house to see what could be found out."

"Nou," Conor said testingly. "Nou."

"One seems to see a curl of the lip, Niall," Banning said lightly and insolently.

"Curl of the soul more likely. Of course, it's not an uncommon Vietnamese name, but I think I'd know the face."

From high above came an interruption. A sudden direct hit on Banning's tweed shoulder, the birdlime in smacking contact sending splashes onto the immaculate pale blue shirt collar. Banning made a strangled sound.

Conor felt Sara inwardly quaking with laughter although her demeanor was grave at this mishap. He said, "Most inconsiderate, seeing that the perpetrator has all twenty-six counties to fly over. Why pick on you?"

He was aware that Banning suddenly and deeply disliked him, and he didn't mind that at all.

Hastily, Sara said, "Let's go and get some decent breakfast. I haven't heard about the boy either—how ghastly whoever he was." And a neat way, Conor concluded, to avoid being left alone with him.

"Gorman, Aloysius Gorman," Banning clarified, in an attempt as an authoritative source to get back his executive standing. "One gathers he was some sort of religious fanatic."

"You mean a Roman Catholic?" Conor asked in bland innocence.

He got a cold and lingering, searching stare. Then Banning snapped his fingers. "Ah—*yes!* The face, the voice. Surely NBC news isn't taking an interest in the not very mysterious death of a lad in an Irish town at the end of nowhere."

"Not unless something—as you might put it—untoward turns up."

Once a month it was Mrs. Broth's custom to summon three young women from Leam to augment her own solitary labors in the care of the house. There would be a perfect storm of dusting, scrubbing, waxing, vacuuming, rug beating, brass and silver polishing. They were married, the three, and were glad to pick up the extra money, particularly as it was understood they could bring their children with them to keep them under their eyes.

"Bottom to top, girls!" Mrs. Broth would command after dispensing early morning tea. "Top to bottom!" This day was usually one when the inhabitants fled the house.

It was hardly the atmosphere for a leisurely breakfast. But Mrs. Broth, who was fond of Conor and delighted to see him, allowed a sit-down meal in the dining room provided Sara cooked it and that they wouldn't linger long. "Or there'll be dust on your bacon, the curtains are to come down, after eight months."

The cleaning corps was in a state of great excitement about last night's death. Details were reiterated to each other from room to room and to anyone who would listen, over pails of foamy water, or an egg cup removed, or a mop stilled in its journey over the parquet of walnut and pearwood.

Conor had been born curious and collected it all. He couldn't understand Banning's lazy interest in a not very mysterious death in a town at the end of nowhere, but perhaps mornings at Dunragh Castle were on the dull side.

Sara only half heard the waves of chatter. She was still feeling as if she had walked into an open elevator shaft and hadn't yet hit bottom.

Conor, from way off and far back, a foot and a half from her, consuming his scrambled eggs.

Ah, God rest him, Wishy Gorman. Poor fellow, his wits were a little skimped anyway and the old mother, That One, hadn't helped with her holy rantings and ravings—a mercy she was dead and wouldn't have to be told about this. (A burst of shrieks and thumps as a four-year-old boy fell over a mop on the stairs and tumbled down on his head, fortunately very close to the bottom.) Harmless, though, Wishy. It was only when he had drink taken that he would march through the town ringing a cracked old bell, denouncing sin and sinners.

Wishy Gorman's wrath fell equally on strong drink, in spite of the fact that indulgence in it inspired his pilgrimages; tobacco, which he was addicted to; the use of drugs, overly short skirts, and what he passionately intoned as "farnication." People listened, smiled, and let him pass unhindered.

He would wind up at St. Agnes' Church, go up the center aisle to the altar rail, and pray loudly for half an hour or so, imploring that the sinners repent. To refresh his memory, and to leave no sin unturned, he would resort to sundry notes and file cards stuffing his pockets. Kind Father Fenn turned a deaf ear to this practice. Sometimes Wishy named names, but as in the course of the years almost everyone in Leam had been mentioned, it was not considered in any way a disgrace to be heard on his list. He had been twenty-eight, it turned out; he looked much younger.

Conor vaguely remembered him as thin and tall, fair-haired and freckled, with huge friendly brown eyes. "Shy as a field mouse when he wasn't shouting his head off," said one of the girls. The day after one of his verbal lambastings—which only occurred once or twice a year—he would meekly return to McCane's, where he was grocery clerk and general helper.

Not encouraged to drink on the premises in the back-room bar, he had left work at his usual six-thirty after sweeping and tidying the store. He usually bicycled home but somebody's car, in the little parking lot beside the grocery, had in the course of fitting itself into a narrow space crushed the front wheel of the bicycle leaning against the pale blue stucco wall. His mother's house, where he still lived and which he now owned, was a mile and three quarters away from the town.

He was seen by a farmer named Ryan, about halfway home, sitting on a stone wall by the road refreshing himself out of a pint bottle of whiskey. "And who'd blame him, the rain falling down on him," Ryan said. "I'd have offered him a lift but I was going the other way, and I was late with my eggs."

"They say a cousin of That One's coming all the way from Letterkenny to see to the funeral," a voice called down the hall outside Upshaw's bedroom. "They say the Garda still have him though, poor Wishy."

Upshaw had been attempting to sleep late. He had had a bad broken night. The sirens and the Garda marching into the house had shaken him severely.

But it wasn't about him at all, it was about somebody else. Stop listening for the sirens, again. "Of course there'll be a post mortem." Ghastly to think about what went on during a post mortem. Don't.

In his sleep, he felt an official hand on his shoulder. "Come along now, you villain." He woke startled and sweating. He had sailed pretty close to it, but never in his life had he been jailed.

A horse, from the stables, whickered. The curtains lifted softly in the night wind and gently fell. The rain had stopped. Not much of a room, this, but the bed was comfortable and the clean sheets smelled sweet. Peaceful here, when you weren't scared to death. What would it be like to live this way as a regular thing?

In the next long wakeful hour, his life sourly reviewed itself for him: shuttling along and about, never finding the right slot. "Or put it this way," Upshaw corrected. "I didn't get the breaks." Carpenter's apprentice, waiter, undergardener, shop attendant, florist's assistant, third barman in a second-rate hotel, guard at the National Gallery, and then bus driver for the Godalmighty C. I. E.

Daylight told him to thrust the fear, the qualms, the cowardice away. This was the one big chance he'd ever had, and if he played it right he might very well turn into a new man going up a broad new road.

But another hour's sleep wouldn't hurt at all.

A smart rap on the door put an end to any hope of that. A handsome dark-haired girl, briefed on the non-importance of this particular visitor by Mrs. Broth, opened the door and put her head in. "Oh, in bed still—sorry, sir, I must do out this room before we're both half an hour older."

Upshaw clutched the sheet to him. "I'll go next door to the bath and then come back here and dress, you can take yourself off until I'm ready."

If only he had a bathrobe. She'd see him draped in his sheet, she'd be giggling behind her hand. But she is merely, he reminded himself, a servant. He went out one door and in the next in a great hurry, and saw not the girl laughing at him but the poodle Peach trotting along with a bone in his mouth.

Returning after a deliberately long hot bath to his bedroom, he dressed and then found that his shoes were not where he was sure he had left them, neatly side by side half under the bed. Maybe in his fright at the sirens he had forgotten to put them back there?

His search started out hurried and ended up frantic. No shoes. Now that he remembered it, his door had been a little ajar when he came back. Had that *dog*—?

Oh Jesus, he thought, this class of thing would never happen to anybody else. And there was a large hole in the toe of one sock.

James's feet as he recalled were narrow. His were wide and flat. And he could never work up the nerve to slip into the lord-of-the-manor's bedroom and try on a pair for size.

Well, steady now. There were two halls and two flights of stairs between here and the ground floor. The dog could have dropped his shoes anywhere along the way.

Around a turn of the landing, he paused and listened, not wanting to be met on the stairs, met and laughed at, by someone coming up. He stared unhappily down at his protruding toe. Linty, saggy, the socks looked, shabby; but he hadn't wanted to wash them out for fear they wouldn't be dry by morning.

Not far below him, he heard the dark-haired girl. "There's pawprints on the down puff in here. Will I dump it outside the door for the cleaning? . . . To think only the night before last he was talking to Mick. He said he was going over to Kilkieran Bay and read the riot act to the *Mary Jean*."

"Who might *Mary Jean* be, a boat?" another voice inquired. "Yes, toss out the puff."

"I suppose so, but Mick says he wasn't making much sense. He'd just been paid and was treating everybody to stout. He'll never get to Kilkieran Bay now God rest him."

A man's voice joining the others now. Conor Niall. "What are you doing with my bedding? And what's this about the *Mary Jean?*"

"It's to be cleaned, Mr. Niall, there's another one in the linen closet, a nice yellow one I'll get out for you . . . a fishing boat I'd think, they're not much for yachts at Kilkieran. But he's missed his final hell and brimstone speech, a waste of voice on that lot— who but the sea gulls would listen anyway?"

"What's this shoe doing here on the stair, Mag? All chewed up. Will I throw it away, or do you suppose the dog will take offense."

"Out with it. Otherwise he'll have a litter of bits and pieces all the way down. It's no good now to whoever owned it."

The voices faded rapidly downward as a crash from what must be the foot of the stairs suggested that a child had knocked over something very large and heavy.

Upshaw started moving again and then stopped. Quite near, below, Bel Kinsella said, "It's his shoe, Upshaw's. Oh God, now he'll never, ever leave." Sounding unlike herself; the high sudden cry.

From Conor Niall, "What? Bel, *what?*"

Nine

In the general commotion of the morning, Upshaw's shoeless entrance upon the scene aroused less attention than he had feared.

Mr. Mamood had just arrived in his Rolls with a veterinarian from Dublin to check Carrowkeel and while he was at it look the horse Belclare over. The veterinarian's name was McKindless O'Brien and he had the imposing looks and height and snowy hair that put one in mind of an eminent surgeon.

Mr. Mamood betook himself with his small cup of hot sweet black coffee to his favorite room, the library. Conor passing by the open door was momentarily amused to see him standing contemplating the large antique globe as though he was turning over in his mind the idea of purchasing continents.

Sara was rescuing white tulips and hyacinths from the runnels of water amid smashed Coalport china on the marble floor of the hall while the cause of the disaster, three years old and brilliantly red-haired, was being alternately scolded and comforted by his mother. Banning stood by clucking his tongue at the loss of such a fine object. "Surely pre-eighteen fifty, I should think."

Conor went down on one knee to help. He said, "This seems like an awfully good place to get out of, right away. Let's go somewhere at a distance and sooner or later find lunch."

"I did love that vase," Sara said. "Oh—thanks, but I'm up to here in work. I must get at it. Will you take charge of these?" She handed him her flowers without exactly looking at him. "Perhaps another day. How long are you staying?" The physical tension between them made the air shake.

"That depends on circumstances," knowing that this was, while reasonable enough on the surface, both a puzzling and a maddening answer.

"Good God, I almost cut myself on that china," said Upshaw's voice over his head. "The dog's taken my shoes. Destroyed at least one of them."

"What size do you wear?" Conor asked, knowing his own foot-gear safe after a glance at Upshaw's socks.

"Nine. At a pinch, if you take my meaning, eight and a half."

"I'd put the case to Mrs. Broth if I were you," Conor advised. "Sara"—catching at her hand as she rose—"work or no, I must talk to you."

She took her hand away. "About what?"

"About Bel." She barely heard him; his head was turned, his eyes following Upshaw through the dining room. "Are you so bound up in yourself and your typewriter and . . ." He decided to omit Fitz. "Can't you see there's something wrong with her, has she been ill, is there anything I haven't been told about?"

"I thought," Sara said slowly, "that it was because somewhere right around now is her wedding anniversary. I didn't like to pry, and bounce merrily around and say, cheer up, dear."

Perhaps. And perhaps the cry torn from her four minutes ago on the landing was not a cry for help at all. Upshaw a nuisance, a social thorn, when she wanted to be with herself and Paul. Walking in white down the aisle of St. Agnes to the tall waiting man at the altar.

Mrs. Broth, whose shoe size was eight and a half, grudgingly supplied Upshaw with her second-best slippers, maroon felt tassled in pink. "You'd hardly like to put on heeled ladies' shoes, and I've only the one pair of sneakers."

Upshaw felt himself at a great disadvantage in the silent shuffling felt slippers. Something must be done about his condition, and right away.

He felt a need to give orders, strike some position, re-establish himself here as a power, a threat. But there were all these women with their mops and brooms and scurrying children. And it didn't take much wit to gather they thought him of little consequence.

"I'll thank you to get out of that chair, Mr. Upshaw, the cover's to be washed."

How could she, Mrs. Kinsella, no, correct this, Bel—how could she *dare?* Complaining about him to her nephew, about how now he would never leave. She'd shut herself off right away. "Sorry,

Conor, wake-up kind of night. Let's go downstairs. I heard the bad news, or some of it, through the door while I was dressing. That poor boy."

But still. "Now he'll never, ever leave." Yes, daring of her. Dangerous of her.

Suddenly attacked by hunger, he went into the kitchen, where at the table McKindless O'Brien was feasting on a plate of ham and eggs, hot whole-meal muffins and butter and marmalade, and a fat brown pot of tea.

To Mrs. Broth, he said, "I've had nothing. Is there . . . ?" He had no idea how to command service and failed dismally now.

"The kitchen," Mrs. Broth said briskly, "is closed. 'Those who lie sleeping have naught for the eating.'" He had never heard this aphorism, but the fact remained that he was to go unfed while O'Brien stuffed himself.

James had come quietly through the butler's pantry. He said, voice gentle, "Mrs. Broth, tea and toast for two, and please leave the tray outside the sitting room. John"—seeming to get the name out with difficulty—"will you join me? Something I wanted to discuss with you."

Nothing to be afraid of, Upshaw told himself as he went with James to the sitting room. Not with this man, whose shyness made him feel almost tongue-tied himself.

For a moment unwilling to broach his subject, James went to a window and looked with loving approval at an explosion of oriental poppies against the tall solemn blue of bearded iris. Very nice together, particularly with the white gyphsophila embroidering the air around them.

Turning, he sighed and said, "It's my understanding that you're waiting here for a check."

Upshaw, standing where he had stood when first stating his business to Bel, in front of the fireplace, took a strong grip on the mantelpiece.

"Yes, I am. That's correct."

"An inconvenience I'd think, especially when you've arrangements to make about a new job."

Was he being led into a trap here? What new job? Oh God yes, the grain and feed store in Ballycastle.

"It's kind of you, but a few days one way or another won't make a difference to the job."

"I've been strapped myself," James said delicately. "I know how it is. I'm prepared to offer you a check, right now, to cover any . . . mmm . . . reasonable needs." He added kindly, forcing the words out, "I'm sure you would do the same for me."

Upshaw's mind raced in circles. Buying him off, getting rid of him? Showing him he wasn't wanted here? Or just sympathy, generosity, of which he had come across very little in his life. Be careful, he thought, there might be a great big hole here for me to step into, and the lid crashing down on my head.

"Thanks, but it happens to be a very large sum—a piece of property of my wife's we've finally disposed of."

"Well then, enough to get you to Ballycastle and keep you in comfort. We'll forward your check as soon as it gets here." James, who seldom smoked, took one of Bel's cigarettes from the pack on the arm of her chair. After lighting it he reached into his pocket for his checkbook.

Hurt feelings rose easily to Upshaw's aid. "As a matter of fact, I came here to pay a visit, which is *why* I asked them to send it to this address in the first place. Am I being told I'm not welcome?"

James, who refused to swat flies and allowed no mousetraps in his room although there were at least two mice in residence there, found himself a battleground. His deep concern about Bel—what had happened to Bel in the last few days, since this man arrived? And on the other hand a strange kind of pity for the man himself, sly and shabby, ridiculous in his pink-tassled slippers; now nakedly showing the wounds of one used to the shame of rejection but never having learned to accept it. What was that phrase? "The insulted and injured . . ."

"It's just that my sister-in-law is not as well as she might be, and the strain of company, however welcome—"

With the determined sullen kicking of a beetle on its back, Upshaw said, "I give no trouble here. I can't even get a bite for breakfast unless it's requested for me by someone she'll listen to. I suppose you're not asking Conor Niall to leave too? Nor Sara Parry. Arabs are allowed, and veterinarians."

James sighed again and thought about appealing to Fitz. Fitz wouldn't dither like this, he would firmly show the man the door if he thought there was a good reason for doing so.

Conor. Conor might offer help of a temporary nature at least. In a tone that signaled the end of their interview, he said, "Well, I just thought I'd make the offer. And I believe I hear a thump which is probably our tray."

"Yes," Conor said ten minutes later. "Yes, glad to, James."

Not an unusual family task. At fourteen, when his Aunt Beatrice came over from Dublin for a week, his mother said on the third day of the visit, "Take her out, *out*. Movies, museums, restaurants, concerts, the park, the zoo, anything. Or I will kill myself. I'll pay you five dollars for each hour she's gone."

Upshaw accepted the offer gratefully. "That's helpful, thank you, Conor." At last a little courtesy, somebody going out of his way for him.

They got into the Morris Minor, which Conor decided could develop engine trouble at any time he chose. An approaching windy thundering made him brake at the near edge of the oval dirt track, a mile long, that encircled the demesne within its walls like a necklace. Carrowkeel being timed by the stopwatch, a great shimmer of speed. A crouching spider of a boy up, his mouth wide with joy and triumph. "Could be dangerous, crossing this track," Upshaw observed almost indignantly. "Very dangerous," Conor agreed.

He proposed driving to Galway for the new shoes, but Upshaw protested. "No, no, they'd be priced out of my reach, wouldn't there be a little shop in Leam?"

Lovely morning, warm and shining; might as well take the long way around. Topping a little rise, he saw to his left a vision from a terrible dream. A girl sprawled, face down, over the low stone wall, her brown hair sweeping a bank of buttercups, blood dripping on them.

It was Agnes Morley's day off and she was hanging out the wash at ten in the morning when she heard, over the fence, about Wishy Gorman's death.

"Fell and brained and drowned himself, apparently," said the Morleys' neighbor Peg, watching Agnes's face with avid curiosity. Wishy was the nearest thing to a boyfriend Agnes had ever had, and vice versa. She was a tall, thin, bony girl with a raw ruddy complexion and anxious apologetic eyes and mouth. Irredeemably plain, except for the long rich brown hair.

The hair fell concealingly over her face as she bent her head, listening to the poured-out embellishments of the story. "A post mortem, isn't that awful now, poor Wishy, and the aunt coming to bury him. Would she be his heir do you think? Though he couldn't have a lot to leave, he was an open-handed spender I'll say that for Wishy."

After Peg retired into her house, Agnes went numbly on with hanging up the sheets and towels, her brother Tom's shirts and her mother's aprons and underwear. She produced no tears and was horrified at herself that at the moment all she could think of, about Wishy, were the poems.

Hands, the aunt's, going through his things, busy hands, sorting, searching. What to be kept, what to be thrown away. Now what's this we have here? *Poems*. Poems to *Wishy?*

"I keep them all, I treasure them," he had told her. "Nobody ever wrote a poem to me before."

And nobody had ever given her chocolates or taken her out bicycling or bought her drinks at a pub before. "Have something grand, Agnes, do, not that old stout—how about some apricot brandy? Or that green peppermint stuff? Refreshing I guarantee you."

She was painfully aware that before Wishy took a shine to her she had been known among her contemporaries as Saint Agnes.

The poems were scribbled off at odd hours as they occurred to her. Two lines, four, six; one had even had three verses. She'd never been much good with her tongue, and it was nice to be able to thank him, in some way, on paper. He was no great speller himself and was uncritical of mistakes.

The most recent one had gone: "A friend like you is far more than money/ And more than a fine dry day or a sweet comb of honey."

She hadn't minded his being taken queer a couple of times a year. In a way it made him something of a celebrity in Leam, and he always got right over it.

How everybody would laugh. Perhaps they'd read the poems aloud, at his wake, for a memorial, and everybody would try to keep, for decency, a straight face. Honest to God, a female Yeats in our midst and we never knew it.

The skin of her face burned. Washbasket emptied, she went into the little house, one of a curving stuccoed row on Market Square. There was a shop at the front, Corson's the Butchers. The Morleys rented the ground-floor kitchen, their main living quarters, and two bedrooms above. In cramped space, there was no possibility of secret comings and goings. Her mother was deaf and wouldn't have heard about Wishy yet. Agnes combed her hair at a cracked mirror over a little cluttered shelf and shouted over her shoulder, "I'm off for air." She ducked out before questions could be asked.

The town looked as it always looked except in the scurry of Market Day. Quiet in the sunlight, as though nothing had happened. She bicycled across the bridge over the River Leam and pedaled hard as the road began to lift gently.

What if his house was locked? Wishy never locked his doors. Would the Garda have been around to see that the house was secured?

The whitewashed thatch-roofed cottage was invisible from the road. Beyond limestone walls a hill went up, topped with rowans, then dipped grassily again to the front half-door. A grown-over track led through a gap in the wall to the cottage.

Not the front door, in case curious people came to look at the place where a man who was living had just died an unexpected death. She left her bicycle tilted against an old twisted apple tree and went around to the back.

A faint wisp of smoke from one of the two chimneys did not alarm her. His faithful turf fire, with the ashes carefully raked over the embers every night, was still keeping his hearth warm for him.

The back door was not quite closed. Silently, feeling suddenly terrified—not of any living thing but of what might remain here, of him, the echo of a voice, of a gay whistling—she pushed the door wider inch by inch. Shadowy light from the windows across the room fell on the hard-packed earth floor, found dim twinkles in a row of flowered jugs on the oak dresser near the fireplace. She had never been inside his house; Wishy didn't think it proper.

He'd surely keep her poems where everybody kept things—wills, insurance policies, birth and marriage certificates, old photographs —in one of the broad top drawers of the dresser.

But what a mess the poor fellow lived in. A stack of newspapers under one window overturned, sheets and blankets flung in a heap in the middle of the floor. She put one foot over the door sill, and then the other. How cold it was. She went toward the hearth with the idea of warming her hands, heard motion behind her, and felt herself struck violently on the back of her head as though by the fist of God.

The first thing she saw when she opened her aching eyes was the earth of the floor, and something big and black and shiny near her—her handbag—with a long curve of silver sticking inexplicably out of the top. With returning consciousness came an almost obliterating wave of terror. Mother of God, she was hurt, she was bleeding, she was maybe dying here in this suddenly evil place.

She struggled to her knees and then to her feet, not even daring to look around. Wait, he might be outside. But no power on earth would keep her inside. She got to the door, watching drops of blood from her head fall onto the floor.

Just over the door sill, she retched and then vomited and almost let it be, let it happen, whatever it was, in her wretchedness. Then, down on one knee, she managed to stand again. An ancient fear did it for her.

Holy Jesus, ghosts couldn't strike in vengeance at you? Life after death . . . he is not dead but liveth. Invading the private place of a man freshly extinguished, not old but young and vigorous, strong, not yet finished with existence one way or another . . .

The bicycle was an impossibility. Wanting concealment, she made her slow way up the slope to the rowans, rested for a time against a bole, and then, helped forward by the tilt of the land, staggered down toward the roadside wall. Dim and dark, it was getting now, clouds across the sun, rain coming?

She woke to a strong arm under her neck, supporting her head, and to a face that was her whole sky now, a remarkable face, especially the eyes, as of someone she had known since early childhood.

"I'll get you all bloodied—"

"That's all right, what's happened to you?"

In perfect trust—rescued as she was from dark places, held and safe and comforted—she said, "I went to get the poems I wrote to Wishy. Aloysius Gorman that is. I was afraid someone would find them. Then I was struck, but by what, or who—"

Lifting his chin, he said over his shoulder, "Look in the glove compartment and see if there's any bottle there."

Upshaw handed him down, not to his great surprise, a pint of Hennessy's on the label of which Jerome had written in his elegant scrawl, "Compliments of the Travelers Aid Society."

The burn of the brandy brought tears to her eyes and patches of sharp color to her cheeks. She tried to sit up. "Oh, but look at your nice jacket arm." The sight of her own blood on the biscuit-colored tweed made her feel ill again, and brought the terror back.

They were all taken by surprise when there was a pound of hooves around the high-banked near curve and in a cloud of lime-stone dust horse and rider pulled up just behind the car.

On the glistening gray's back was a man Conor had no trouble in identifying. Slim and compact, gracefully erect. Well-made face with skin of poreless olive-gold satin, large dark flashing eyes, crisply trimmed dark mustache, and fashionably cut hair to match. Mid-fifties, must be, although he didn't look it. Heavy ivory linen hacking jacket, whipcord breeches, tattersall shirt, boots with the sheen of chestnuts.

He asked no unnecessary questions and uttered no exclamations of astonishment. "Is the wound bad? She'll need a doctor in any case—I'm not a quarter of a mile away from here. Suppose we get her there right away." His only accent was that he was carefully without any accent at all, giving attention to each separate word he spoke.

It was an obviously sensible suggestion with which Conor could find no quarrel. He and Upshaw lifted the girl into the back of the car. She was shivering now and Conor picked up a folded blanket from the floor and wrapped it hurriedly around her.

Turning his horse in the direction he had come from, General Nou said, "You'll be all right in no time, Agnes—isn't it?" And to the two men, "She works at Dunragh."

Banning had been reporting into his tape recorder for several minutes before the Morris Minor came up the long drive.

"There is this I can only say rather dreadful little man, John Upshaw by name, who arrived three days ago at Leam House. About five-eight, early forties, muddy skin, brown hair and eyes, nobody one would glance at twice. Suit off the rack, a general Woolworth air about the rest of his furnishings. Slight lisp or something that sounds like it. Is not in a proper family bedroom but has been placed in a maid's room. Had a closed-door conference shortly after his arrival with Mrs. Kinsella who is said not to have been herself since. Purported to be a distant relative, a step-cousin of sorts, which would of course explain his presence here to the casual eye, or ear.

"Conor Niall arrived the evening following Upshaw's entrance upon the scene. He is a correspondent, or whatever term they use, with NBC news." Banning paused here and frowned. Conor Niall's dark amused fineness had for a few minutes stripped him of something, some confidence, assurance, power. "According to my source in New York, he is looked upon as one of their future big boys and is now going into feature work for them on and off, investigative reporting and so on. This is his first visit to Ireland in a year and a half. He is a perfectly genuine relative—son of Mrs. Kinsella's sister. What follows may have no bearing whatever on the matter, but I thought it might amuse you. This morning he was discovered by self in what might be called a passionate embrace—standing up and clothed, I didn't mean to say *that* passionate—with Sara Parry, who seemed somewhat unwilling to return his ardor. One wonders what Fitz would think if he had seen it, or was told about it by some malicious personage."

The window of his study was open. Below, he heard the approaching car and under the engine noise a horse's trotting. He put his head out and looked down at the car, its top folded back and its passengers highly visible.

Over a tremendous whack of the heart, "Well, great heavens," said Banning to himself. Hands suddenly chilled and inept, he put the tape recorder into a cabinet over his desk and turned the key in the lock.

What in Christ? Right here on the doorstep, here are the subjects. With some injured blanket-wrapped young woman who looked familiar even with her hair all over her face. Of course,

Agnes Morley. Now, what was Agnes Morley doing here on her day off?

Back to the window again. Nou's collected demeanor as he dismounted and went to help with Agnes told the stunned watcher that there was, after all, no immediate cause for alarm.

Ten

"Police?" asked General Loc Nou with a slow blink of his dark eyes. "Oh, you think it's a police matter?"

Agnes Morley had been efficiently taken over by what seemed to be the male housekeeper, a Vietnamese, with assurances that she would be put to bed. Dr. Quin from Leam was on the way. The four men, Banning listening intently on the edge, were in a windowed corner of one of Dunragh Castle's immense reception rooms. This stone cavern with twenty-foot ceilings was not only warmed as well as might be by central heating, but it offered fires at both ends, a great splendor of lemon and green and sapphire silk brocades, Chinese carpets which clearly stated their price-lessness, and little islands of sumptuously comfortable sofas and chairs.

Conor remembered Dunragh from his childhood, a delightfully terrifying place to play. Dark, cold, mysterious, crumbling, with interior pools of water under broken towers. He and Fitz had had a game of shouts, one trying to trace the echoes through rooms and passages and up and down stairways to find where the other had shouted from.

He pulled himself back from a tenth of a second's journey to a forgotten universe of time; back to the luxurious, transformed Dunragh present. "She said she was struck. In Gorman's cottage."

"I don't know where I'd gotten the idea that your car had hit her as she crossed the road. That blind curve is bad." He looked and sounded entirely sincere.

"No," Conor said. "It didn't."

Another Vietnamese in a surgically white coat came in with a tray of biscuits, coffee, and sherry.

"Gorman?" asked Nou, narrowing one eye as if to summon a recollection that wasn't there.

"The boy who came to an unfortunate end last night," Banning supplied. "A misstep in the rain. Drowned in Kinsellas' stream."

"How sad."

Death is his milieu, Conor thought, death in multiples. It must be difficult to manage even polite concern.

"But he is not—what is the phrase—already laid out in his cottage?"

"No, she must have had an errand there." For some reason he chose not to mention her seeking her poems, which had to him a wrenching ring of truth.

"By all means, call the Garda, Calvin."

To Nou's offer of refreshment from the tray, Conor said, "No thank you." Upshaw, looking around him, far out of his depth, mumbled that he would like a glass of sherry.

Dr. Quin arrived, an obsequious—at least in this place—small man with a lock of red-gray hair falling between his eyebrows. Go ahead, pull it, Conor said silently.

"I've ordered the ambulance from Costelloe just in case. We'll want X rays no matter what we find. And now if I may see my patient?"

Would there have been an ambulance ordered for a head wound in a common house?

Upshaw noticed the General's gaze on his maroon slippers. He explained hastily, "We were off to Leam for shoes for me—the dog destroyed mine—when we came across that young woman lying over the wall."

Nou beckoned the tray-bearer, now waiting near towering folding doors for any command, and whispered to him. Five minutes later, the man brought a choice of three pairs of shoes for Upshaw to try on, all expensive and in shining condition. "Muddy here occasionally," Nou explained. "I keep fresh shoes for my guests when needed." Finding a pair, black, which fitted him perfectly, Upshaw said, "I couldn't possibly, General." "Think nothing of it," said Nou. Upshaw, thinking that this was perhaps a Far Eastern custom when entering a palace, gratefully accepted his St. James's Street footgear.

Conor violently wanted out, but he felt it a duty to wait to hear the state of Agnes Morley.

Re-entering, Quin said, "Ten stitches, very neat if I say so my-self. But now for the X ray."

"Should she then be taken home?" Banning asked.

"Home? With the mother deaf and the brother drunk and she here with a grand good bed and care the clock around? And when she wakes up well and strong again, it's her day to go back to work anyway she tells me, although with a good kind man like the General—" Anxious, no doubt, to maintain this new contact with Dunragh Castle and display his medical skills; Nou and Banning would probably bestow their ailments on Dublin specialists.

"Of course," Nou said. "While we're waiting for the ambu-lance, have a glass of sherry, doctor. Calvin—do call Mrs. Morley. Raise your voice. Tell her there's no danger of any sort. Is that the police I hear?"

It was. To the two young Gardai Conor had met the night be-fore in the kitchen, he gave a brief summary of his encounter with Agnes, again omitting the poems.

Sergeant Grady scowled ferociously. "Some low-down scuttler, maybe, bound on robbery now the poor fellow's gone."

The four men left the castle together, Upshaw carrying Mrs. Broth's slippers in a paper sack which had been discreetly pro-vided.

It was only later that Conor heard what the police immediately found at the cottage: Agnes's large black plastic handbag, left behind on the floor. It contained jammed-in pound notes as well as the small sum tucked neatly into her own wallet; a ring set with a small and not very valuable diamond; a tie clip that looked like gold but probably wasn't; and what was obviously a handed-down family treasure, a Georgian silver soup ladle, its long curving han-dle patterned with lilies.

The cottage showed every sign of a hurried untidy search. And on one corner of the dresser there was a smear of blood with a long brown hair caught in it.

"I'd say someone surprised her at it and gave her a shove and she hit the dresser and knocked herself out," Sergeant Dall theorized. "And she, supposed to be his girl, at that. We'll go back and have a chat as soon as she's able to raise her head from the pillow and give an account of herself."

Upshaw's seediness was in a way a relief, at least for a few minutes, after the prosperous lethal shine of General Nou.

"Well," Conor said, heading toward the coast, "you must have wonderful stories to tell about the sisters and the uncles and the cousins and the aunts. Catch me up on how we're connected."

Upshaw didn't like the hard inquiry behind the amiable words. "Where are we going? Does this take us back to the house?"

"I thought I'd show you something of the countryside. Without a car you've been more or less trapped I suppose. You wouldn't want to miss the cliffs while you're here."

Now decently shod, Upshaw encountered another disadvantage. With the top down, the car created its own wind, which blew his hair down over his forehead and into his eyes, not contributory to his dignity.

"One family's very like another," he said, trying without success to control his hair with his hand. "I wouldn't want to be away too long, I may be getting a call from the feed and grain fellows."

"Oh yes, and that check of yours. We'll just take a quick run." In the manner of a tour guide, Conor talked vivaciously of Lough Corrib, "best free-fishing in the country. Salmon and trout enough to get in the way of your boat." And the glories of Westport House at Clifden. "You can see the Twelve Bens, or Twelve Pins, take your choice, just after we round this bend. Lovely, aren't they? Never the same color second to second." And Carna, on the promontory between Bertraghboy and Kilkieran bays, the center for Connemara ponies. "Nice little beasts. Did you ride one as a boy?" The unkindness of this last startled him; Upshaw seemed to bring out a new worst side of himself.

He was well aware that his captive audience was both nervous and bored.

While he talked, some trained machine in his head was delicately ticking, working, probing, in a way he was hardly aware of.

Wishy Gorman, casually dead. "He said he was going over to Kilkieran Bay and read the riot act to the *Mary Jean*." *Mary Jean? Mary Jean?* "But he's missed his final hell and brimstone speech." "I went to get my poems I wrote to Wishy. Then I was struck, but by what or who?"

Passing rapidly through Costelloe, he drove north to Screeb, turned west and then south to Kilkieran Bay. Upshaw had given up protesting for the moment. Now all he asked of his Creator was a pint of stout, or a double whiskey, or both. He suggested a pub and Conor said, "I know just the place, nice little town on the bay."

The town of Ilch had always reminded him of Provincetown; he supposed fishing villages all over the world had family resemblances. The cheerfully untidy piers, the sea gulls, the shouts and laughter heard through the clear air. The rocking litter of boats tied up or busily coming and going, the smell of Diesel fuel and ancient ground-in fish flakes. The bright wind-floated washlines strung between gaily colored if dilapidated houses stacked up the hill from the bay.

The Kestrel's Rest, the waterside pub, was clean and sunny and roaring with trade.

Before his visit to the men's room, the little ticking machine in Conor's head gave him an order which he promptly obeyed. "Get me another and ask the bartender if he knows whether the *Mary Jean* is in port."

If there is anything in this, and if anyone is going to go looking for trouble because of it, the machine had decided, it might as well be Upshaw, not me.

Taking this opportunity to request and down a double whiskey and then ask for two more pints of lager, Upshaw inquired of the blue-jawed man behind the bar, "Would there be do you know a boat named the *Mary Jean* in port?"

The man paused with his hand on the pump and considered. "There's the *Mary Ann,* and the *Mary Mother,* but—well, let's see now." He raised his voice. "Any of you lads know about a boat called the *Mary Jean?* This fellow wants to know if she's tied up here."

Conor, returning, felt as he passed through at least one pocket of sudden silence in the crowded smoke-teeming bar.

The *Mary Jean* had presented itself to him back there on the road as a ridiculously and dangerously clear code name for marijuana and/or drugs of any kind. And because so readable, probably never used openly, just among one's own associates on the quiet.

The two words seemed to linger ringing in the air.

Upshaw felt vaguely uncomfortable. That great red-faced lout on one of the leather-cushioned benches staring at him, huge hairy hand holding his pint close to his chest.

"There's no such boat around here I know of," said a blue-eyed blond boy with a look of uncomplicated truth about him. "Maybe from up the coast somewhere. Have you tried Kilkieran?"

They did try Kilkieran, a pub this time named the Tug of War, Upshaw again required to place the question. Good God, Upshaw thought, a weak bladder is it, in a well set-up man of his age?

There was a *Rosemary,* and a *Mary Come Home,* but the *Mary Jean* appeared to be unknown in Kilkieran too. Conor, scanning faces as the matter was lengthily discussed, gave up. Irish faces were not easy to read. That saturnine hawk of a man might be the village saint; that pink-faced boy with pale red hair and dimples might be embroiled up to his dainty small flat ears in secret crime.

It was now close to two o'clock. They chose roast beef sandwiches from a well-filled rack. Conor lingered over his, said he'd have another, and spent some more time over a dish of apple pudding he didn't want.

Upshaw kept glancing at his watch. "We've at least an hour's run before we get back—"

"Yes, and that's if the car holds up," Conor said cheerfully. "I thought it sounded a little odd coming down the hill here. That's the worst of borrowed cars, you don't know their special groans and grunts."

He decided aloud that the engine did need looking at, just as they were conveniently approaching Screeb. He pulled into an Exxon station. "I don't know what's wrong with it, it sounds queer though," he said to the mechanic. "Give it a going over, will you? No hurry."

Upshaw got out of the car sulkily. He was thinking, She could be off and away by now. Maybe this is all planned. James with his offered check. And now Conor Niall holding him—the word prisoner came into his mind, and he felt unseen handcuffs and heavy chains.

I've let it go long enough, he told himself. As soon as we get back I'll put the real pressure on.

He bought a can of Fanta at a dispensing machine and leaned against the back of the car drinking it lugubriously.

Like his brothers everywhere, the mechanic in a leisurely way tried to find out not what was right but might be profitably wrong with the car.

Good, Conor thought, more power to you. No hurry at all. The house at Leam gratefully emptied of Upshaw; Agnes Morley in a soft bed at Dunragh Castle, no doubt supplied with nourishing broth and tea and toast—

No hurry? Still following instinct without tracing its exact source, he went to the telephone kiosk at the edge of the service station's concrete apron, collected a few coins from his pocket, and dialed.

Sara's television project for Telefis Eirann was a series of six half-hour scripts based on the short stories of her celebrated grand-uncle, Liam St. Leger Parry.

She had been chosen for the assignment not because of family ties but because she had shown herself in her work in Hollywood as having an extraordinary touch with dialogue, mood, and character.

She was working on "The Rathmullan Donkey" when she was interrupted. *Thump.* There was joy and demand in the signal on her door, although the edge of the fist was light. She got up from her typewriter, glanced at herself in a mirror, and opened the door.

"Here I come, ready or not," said Fitz, and put his arms around her. "This close," he murmured, "you ought to be able even to feel the check in my pocket. Not just Carrowkeel, but Belclare. Have you any champagne on ice?"

"Two splits, I think, will that do?"

"Nicely. I'll get it."

Feeling herself unnervingly turned into two women, she went again to the mirror to see who, exactly, she was. Behind and over her head in the glass, her future seemed to be hanging in the room, in the stream of sun, like drifting pollen and motes in the golden air.

Nonsense. Other people, places, atmospheres, didn't decide things for you. You decided them for yourself.

Fitz came back with two filled and fizzing glasses. "Not really to the horses," he said, touching his to hers. "To us."

He drank off half his glass, put it down, and took both her hands.

"I wish," he sighed, "that I could take your clothes off and then my own, but I keep having this feeling that a horse will put its head through the window. Or Upshaw will come around trying to borrow five pounds. Or James will want to present you with a bouquet of something or other. Right in the middle of things."

He seemed anything but alarmed and tentative. His red-brown skin was glowing and his brown eyes were full of light. In his riding clothes, he looked not at all on stage, but perfectly himself and marvelously removed from the commonplace.

And that feeling that she had known him—known him really well, down into the bone—not just for five weeks but for a long, long time. Don't, at the moment, try to define the sense of sweet familiarity. Don't complicate what must, in order to be right for both of them, be quite direct and simple.

What a relief, what a release commitment would be. This is it, you and no other. In a strange paradoxical way it would mean getting herself back, all of herself, after a year and a half of painful ambivalence.

"Hell and damnation," Fitz said mildly as the telephone five feet away rang.

It was Conor. "Sara, did I snatch you away from anything?"

"No." As if he could, literally interpreted in the context of the moment.

"I know this is an odd request, but would you—? No, I'd better start again. There's a girl, Agnes Morley, at Dunragh. She's had a head injury. We found her this morning and took her there. I'm a little worried about her. Could you drift over with a book or some flowers and make known your, let's see, interest in her well-being?"

For some reason the request outraged her—dispatched by him on gray-lady errands. Where *was* he? He couldn't know Fitz was here, could he? Was this some highhanded interference?

"My once and future Sara."

Controlling her voice, she said, "Sorry, but I am as usual a couple of days behind. In any case, I'm going over there to tea, a few hours from now, I will ask about her if you like."

After several seconds of silence, "Okay, Sara. Do ask." Buzz.

Conor gone. Too late to change her mind even if she wanted to.

"That was Conor, wasn't it?" Fitz asked. His face had gone a deeper color with sudden and open rage. "What did he want of you that you were sorry you couldn't do?"

"Some sick-visiting, some protégée of his hurt apparently." She had heard about Fitz's temper; now she felt the hot strong gust of it coming at her.

"The gall of him! Arranging your afternoons for you! I must tell him at the first opportunity to keep his fingers out of my pies. And I wish"—eyes very dark and penetrating now, looking at her in a way to cause discomfort—"he'd get to hell away from here, and from you, and back to his bloody cameras."

Conor had, whatever his intentions, shattered some mood, some inevitable and intoxicating pattern of words and action, in which minds were made up and matters were settled. Settled with tidiness, with passion.

"I'll be off to the bank before it closes," Fitz said, outwardly brisk again. "This will be very good news to anyone there who might be worrying about our overdraft."

Nou, in the manner of Richard Nixon but in no way inspired by him, had listening devices in his own nest; in fact, throughout Dunragh. The mutter of one guest to another in a quiet corner; servants' chatter; invaluable.

Banning's study was in the technical word clean. In midafternoon, Nou away at a meeting in Galway of the Landmarks Preservation Board, he addressed himself again to his tape recorder. He kept his voice orderly and calm. It was part of his self-image to register as imperturbable.

"At one-ten on eighth June Niall and Upshaw arrived at the Kestrel's Rest pub in Ilch. Upshaw inquired of the bartender as to whether the *Mary Jean* was in port. He made no attempt at secrecy, the whereabouts and/or existence of the boat were taken up by the other patrons. The two men went on to Kilkieran, where Upshaw asked the same question, again openly. Upon leaving Kilkieran, they drove east along the bay and stopped at an Exxon station where the car, a green Morris Minor convertible, is at present, the time now being three-seventeen. The station mechanic is still working on it. Note: we have long since ordered dropping the use of that name, but habits die hard, particularly among the unlettered.

"Agnes quiet now, as well she should be." Banning stopped and thought for a moment. But, simple. Men of the world handled a given matter on two, three different levels. In any case, nobody but Nou would hear the tape. Why then the faint far lightning flare of worry? Nonsense.

"Sergeants Grady and Dall talked to her at one P.M. Grady wanted to let it go until tomorrow, but Dall insisted on the interview. I was not present but nearby. They informed her of the stolen goods and money discovered in her handbag at Gorman's cottage. Her reaction was predictable. Furious denials, then torrents of tears. Grady heard to say, 'Lashing about in that way you'll be tearing your stitches out. Calm down, Agnes, do.' Her excuse for being at the cottage, what sense could be made of it, was that she was looking for some poems she had written. Now I ask you. The Garda men on leaving said they would be wanting to talk to her again tomorrow. She, of course, then required strong sedation. The rest of the staff was ordered to stay away from her room and maintain absolute quiet if and when they passed the door."

Sara, without enthusiasm, drove herself over to Dunragh at five o'clock. She should have refused when she was first invited, pleading work, but it was too late now.

The corkscrew road had to be taken slowly. Its hedges were fuchsias, a dozen feet high, just coming into bloom. The air was warm and gentle. A small orchestra of thrushes tuned up around a bend striped in sun and shadow. It was, she supposed, a fine thing to be liberated, to be invited singly to the castle for the pleasure and flavor of one's own company; none of that outdated business of a man as escort. But it would be nice, on this lovely afternoon, to have one's own man—yes, Fitz, beside her. It would be a party, not an obligation.

Tricky, getting past three parked tinkers' caravans, although they were pulled as close as possible to the hedges. Two of them red, one yellow. Glimpses through the open backs of domestic comforts, a flash of mirror, a glow of brass, an armchair with a pink-and-white-flowered slipcover. Advantage had been taken of the sun to get the washing done. It was flung brilliantly over the hedges to dry.

Beyond the great white wrought-iron gate, hospitably open, Dunragh's locally famed rhododendrons towered on either side of the drive. Leaves glistening as though individually hand-polished, great blossoms flushed with their own light, mauve and fragile pink and incandescent white.

Too bad, she thought again, to be alone, in this brief timeless fairytale. It had, delightfully, nothing to do with the real world. White peacocks on the lawn, a breeze stirring the roses in immense ivory-golden marble urns flanking the shallow stone steps leading up to the broad terrace. She stopped midway up, breathing the scented air, wanting a hand in hers, familiar and strong, to double the sweetness.

She had been watched for. The carved door of black bog oak was swinging open. Calvin Banning, pale and with his cheeks oddly shaking, stood just inside. From behind him, she got a confused impression of stage noises: running feet, a telephone ringing, a distressed shriek from some remote chamber.

"I'd say come in, but you'd be better off going home," he said. "I've just this past few seconds called the police. My God. Dead."

Conor? *Conor?* Wild immediate thought, perhaps because of the essential hand she had been holding, walking up between the roses.

"Who?"

"Agnes Morley. She's a maid here." He touched his damp forehead with a fastidious finger, took out a handkerchief and wiped it dry. "Apparently took a bundle of Darvon from the cabinet in the bathroom between the two rooms—been told she'd be fine in twenty-four hours and then goes and— but I suppose that interview with the police, the disgrace— sorry, I'm not making sense."

Her own voice came back to her in the silence. Her answer to Conor, who said he was a little worried about Agnes Morley, and would she go over with a book or some flowers and inquire as to the girl's well-being.

Politely cool, "I'm going over there to tea." Politely grudging, "I will ask about her if you like."

Eleven

At about three thirty in the afternoon, in her bedroom, Bel briefly contemplated suicide.

She stood looking at the articles collected on her bed. Dismiss the bits and pieces, the little single-strand pearl bracelet, the rings, the diamond hoop earrings. Her emerald necklace, a fifteenth-anniversary present from Paul might bring—how much? Jewelers were discreet, used to women in dire straits slinking in and laying down their treasures with trembling hands. Not new, but jewels and gold didn't age like their wearers. Surely the necklace ought to cover it?

Yes, I know, Paul, this is betrayal pure and simple. Instead of saying to myself, to Upshaw, it can't be true, just go away, will you? I am agreeing that there is something, something that has to be covered up, something about you, dark.

For a terrifying moment she found herself trying to grasp his identity; to find out who, really, Paul Kinsella had been. This shabby man had managed, almost, to take her husband away from her. It was like a second death, a second bereavement. Only, which one of them was now coffined?

Concentrate. If the jeweler said, "No thank you, madame, we're very well stocked with emeralds," her furs might raise some money. A two-skin Russian crown sable loop, almost new, a present from Fitz when he'd just sold Glenamoy. A pearl-buttoned, back-belted coat of pale golden mink, eight years old but fresh and softly gleaming. A great ten-foot length of cloudy, downy blue fox she had liked to wear with evening things, going partying with Paul.

"Naturally, madame, as these furs are used their value is vastly diminished. For the three pieces, we are prepared to offer—" Ten thousand pounds? Hardly.

Upshaw would suspect, if she went to Dublin to sell the goods on the bed, that she was running away. He would insist on accompanying her. And no doubt join in the bargaining with the furrier, the jeweler, trying to squeeze up the price.

Fitz had told her, after lunch, about the check in his pocket. One hundred and twenty thousand pounds. And she couldn't ask him for tenpence of it. Of course, a lot would be requisitioned for the stables, and there would be tax, and he had said their overdraft at the bank was impressive.

Leam House, with its five hundred acres, was in her name. There was that large unused stretch across the road from the back gates. How much would that bring? But there would be people coming to look at it, lawyers, papers, witnesses to signatures. The selling of it would be a public and limelit affair. "What's got into you, selling our land, Mother?" What, in fact, amounted to, in not so many years, his land.

Better to rely for the moment on her personal possessions. For the moment. Upshaw had implied that this would not be the end of it. What was to stop him—once she had said yes, all right, I'll go along with you—from applying to her every year, or twice a year?

She looked into the long cold black tunnel of the future. Was she to spend the rest of her life like this, scheming and scraping and cowering?

There was, of course, an alternative. There must be at least two dozen sleeping pills in the bathroom.

The ultimate sin, the Church said: despair. But who, in full possession of his faculties, ever announced firmly to himself, "Now then. I am going to submit to despair."

A calm, peaceful death the sleeping pills would arrange for her. Or—out of it by then, would you froth and dribble? Would your nose run? Would the late Isobel Kinsella be a loved woman sadly gone forever, or a present and glaring atrocity?

It occurred to her that it was amazing what vanity could do. When you peered around a corner at death, vanity held up a mirror. It nudged you, stepped on your toes, made you think, Well, I don't know, after all . . .

Perhaps not vanity alone.

Who would see to it that James ate his lamb chop and took his pills?

And the lime trees were just beginning to toss white high bloom in the wind and send their perfume in at doorways and windows.

And possibilities had not been entirely extinguished. There was Conor. Not that Conor could take over, wave Upshaw away. It was not just the man himself who had to be dealt with, it was a set of facts, times, places, people. It was a photograph in a pocket.

But it was nice that Conor was *there*. Strong and able, and at an emotional remove from the matter, even though he had been so fond of Paul.

After the money had been paid, Conor might be turned to, confided in. He could try to see that Upshaw didn't come round again. Threaten him with bodily damage or exposure. Make him write a note. "You can keep the money and forget a prison sentence if you write the following: 'I know of no facts pertaining to the late Paul Kinsella. I have never heard of the man.'"

Of course he could never, never be asked to help her to get rid of Upshaw in some unnamed and unthinkable way.

Bel was not by nature a door-closer. Her bedroom door was ten inches open. James came along the hall on his way to his room for a nap. He saw her reflection in the cheval glass in the corner, hands in the immemorial clasp of supplication, of woe, against her breastbone. He read the hands and the taut white face with the insight of a man who had been silently and undeviatingly in love with her for thirty years.

He was shaken with rage. They—*he*—cannot be allowed to do this to you, Bel, whatever it is. I will get you out of it, no matter how, no matter what.

No nap now, of course, but stretch out on the bed and try to rest and quiet the racing heart. He would need a clear head, and such strength as in the face of acute emergency he could summon.

The double-horse van containing Carrowkeel and Belclare, with a boy named Coney in back to keep them company and his brother driving, left Leam House at three thirty, bound for Shannon Airport.

Trahey felt, seeing them safely off, a great sense of loss and at the same time a surge of celebration. He thought of them as his horses in a way; it was he who had trained them to their wind-sweeping perfection.

He retired to his quarters over the west wing of the stables, took off his boots and his sweater, got out a bottle of Niall's, and prepared for the sort of relaxation he seldom allowed himself in midafternoon.

His old cracked leather chair by the window was deep and comfortable. After his first gulp, he held his glass up to the light and said aloud, "To you, Mr. Trahey." There would be a handsome check from Fitz, a well-earned bonus. Not that he needed the money any more; hadn't this past thirteen months. But it was pleasant to feel appreciated.

No road work tonight. Everything before him free and clear. The one cloud on the horizon being that fellow Upshaw. He couldn't himself see what all the worry about Conor Niall was. The man was after all a nephew, part of the family, why wouldn't he pay a visit if he had the time and the money?

But, the other. He began to brood on Upshaw. What the *hell* was he doing here? The information he, Trahey, had passed along didn't tell any of them very much. A relative who looked as if he wasn't one. Prowling around, peering secretly into windows, having closed-door interviews with Mrs. Kinsella. Stowed in a maid's room like some kind of underling or some kind of sneaking scurrilous official.

Trahey refilled his glass. He was not a patient or subtle man. He believed in getting, or plunging, to the bottom of things whenever he was puzzled or worried.

It was a tempting idea to face up to Upshaw, give him a bad fright, and send him scuttling back to whatever dark burrow he had emerged from. It might prove a point too.

If he was official trouble, he would stand his ground. If unofficial trouble, he might dodge and run.

After finishing his second drink he went to the house and in at the kitchen door. Mrs. Broth was arranging a small plate of her Tidbits. She placed a slice of water chestnut on a little pat of wine-streaked cheese and topped the chestnut with a plump white truffle.

"Mrs. Kinsella couldn't get down any lunch," she said indignantly over her shoulder. "Of course the house is turned upside down, but normally that wouldn't put her off."

As if following her mental processes, Trahey asked, "Where's that fellow Upshaw?"

"Conor's taken him off in his car. Up Conor, I say."

"Ring me out there when they get back, will you?"

She gave him an odd glance, and something like a smile hovered about her mouth. Yes, she would be glad to.

The Morris Minor pulled in a little after five thirty. Upshaw all but leaped out of it in his eagerness. Suppose he had been right, suppose she had taken the opportunity to pack her bag and flee? And the story put about that they had no idea where she'd gone. She'd just taken it into her head that she wanted a change.

"Where's Mrs. K.?" he immediately inquired of Mrs. Broth, who was thoughtfully sipping her first glass of sherry. The commotion of women and china and glass at the double sinks produced a sense of conversational privacy.

"Mrs. Kinsella, if that's who you're asking for, is busy in her room writing letters. I see you've finally got shoes on. Where are my slippers?"

"In the car." The second pressing question rushed to his lips. "What about the horses, are they sold?" If they were, there must be a fairly tremendous sum of money within touching distance. Or promised, anyway, in the very near future.

"I've been busy with the house. I have no idea as to the daily business of the stables," Mrs. Broth said loftily. Then inspiration struck her. "Why don't you go and take a look? I'd say if they were gone, they were sold, wouldn't you?" She called the stable number the moment Upshaw went out the door.

The unwelcomed tour of the countryside had eaten up the cream of the day as far as weather went. Now the skies were beginning to darken and there was a green smell of approaching rain. Upshaw cautiously crossed the track on the soft turf just behind the starting gates, although there wasn't a horse within sight or hearing.

He felt confused and apprehensive. The air, maybe, heavily pressing now. Or the sudden whickering in a stall eight feet from his ear, which made him jump. Over and above these things, an uneasy feeling that he wasn't able to get his fingers on an item that might be important, might be essential.

Was Mrs. K. planning to escape on the *Mary Jean?* Was that why they had devoted so much time to trying to find her? What the hell did a man from the States, a television man, have to do with an Irish fishing boat?

If she went out to sea, there would be no way to get at her.

The nerve of him, Conor Niall, trying to locate the boat right under my nose, Upshaw thought. *If* that's what the *Mary Jean's* wanted for.

To calm himself, he stopped to light a cigarette. Well, she wasn't the only one concerned. He could always go straight to the son. Men, though, a different matter. Fists, force, to say the least. Obviously, she hadn't told Fitz, hadn't told James; he'd see the knowledge, and what they thought of him for it, in their faces. But she might have told a nephew who wasn't exactly part of the family, whom disgrace wouldn't particularly touch.

There were brass name plates on the stalls that faced out onto the courtyard contained within the length and two wings of the stable building. Sixteen stalls in all. The two labeled Carrowkeel and Belclare were empty.

Out being exercised? Certainly not both of them at once—too much of a coincidence. Immense sums floated before Upshaw's eyes. He might be out and away from here tonight, or at the latest tomorrow morning.

There was the sound of a heel on stone behind him. He swung and faced Trahey, two feet away. Yellow hair on his flat-topped head tossed about, icy-blue chips of eyes under the inflamed red rock of forehead.

Trahey's voice was low and thick. He was halfway drunk but saw no harm in pretending he was more so.

"Good day, Mr. Upshaw. Just by happy chance the man I wanted to see."

Assert yourself before this stablehand. "How much did they bring?"

"Did what bring?"

"The horses the Arab bought."

"Let's see," Trahey said, frowning as though in concentration. "Carrowkeel, five pounds, and Belclare, two-and-six."

"Look here—" began Upshaw, choking with rage.

Trahey picked up a pitchfork leaning next to Carrowkeel's stall.

"It's for you to look here." Swaying a little, he bent and touched the long shining tines.

"Wicked things, these can be," he said. "Fellow in Moycullen got a man with one of these, a man he caught stealing his sheep. Of course he'd taken a drop and maybe didn't know what he was doing. First the face, and then . . . *Jesus.*"

A shock of fear stabbed Upshaw in the bowels. But it was broad daylight, and he was within shouting distance of the house. Or was he? It was very still. Not even the sound of a bird. Just the other man's heavy breathing.

"It's my understanding that you'll be leaving this place in"— Trahey considered briefly—"twenty-four hours. Is that correct?"

"What's correct is that when I leave here is none of your bloody business." But he backed away several feet.

Trahey struck the pointed tines of the pitchfork against the stones underfoot. They gave out a sharp clarion ringing. He smiled, showing his small bad teeth. "Of course, I may be taking chances brandishing this thing in front of you. Maybe in your line of work you carry a gun."

Bewilderment was added to Upshaw's anger and fear. What line of work? Or was Trahey out-and-out referring to him as a criminal?

He could turn and walk away, but right at the moment he didn't want to present his back to this drunken lout.

"Maybe around this stable a man ought to," he said.

"Ah well, then, agreed, twenty-four hours it is." Trahey flung the pitchfork from him. It neatly pierced a bale of hay. "That fellow, that sheep stealer, lived in spite of it all, but in ways you'd think he'd wish he hadn't." He turned away, the smile widening into a savage grin. "Enjoy the rest of your stay, Mr. Upshaw."

I can't, I can't, Sara said to herself, I can't face him.

Not with this girl's—what is her *name?*—death right here all over my hands.

Anywhere but back to the stone cottage, and the creamy house in its circlet of water, and Conor.

In Paul's old but staunch dark red Mercedes, she turned right as she went through the Dunragh gate and was passed by the Garda Rover arriving in full cry. The Rover made it real. It had actually happened. Banning had stood in the doorway with his cheeks trembling and said, "My God. Dead."

Quickly, through the quiet town. Not McCane's bar. She had had a drink there once and been looked at by several dozen men as if she was an invader, and scarlet at that. Her grip on the wheel was rigidly tight, as though it was something to hang onto, a badly needed support.

Slowing for a dusty ramble of chickens, she remembered a pub Fitz had taken her to a few weeks back, high on a hill to the west of the town on the road to Glasna. Glasna was where the Garda station was. And where when your mind was not on police matters you could amuse yourself buying the handloomed powder-weight tweeds that placed the town on the shopper's map.

The pub was called the Queen of Corrib. Several of its windows looked down at the great islanded sweep of the Lough. It was full enough to provide fiercely necessary human company, but she found a little booth all to herself where at the window beside it was a painted wooden box of burning blue-purple cineraria. Opposite the window, not far away, a green hill shot eerily straight up. She claimed her booth with her yellow-and-white striped scarf tossed on the table and went to the bar and ordered a double whiskey. For some reason, she said, "Jameson's, please."

She was looked at casually, but there were other well-dressed attractive people there. Lots of money around, Fitz had said, foxhunting territory, long weekend parties, and even in this many-laked countryside indoor and outdoor swimming pools.

Taking her Jameson's to the booth, she sat and looked at it and tried to do something about her mental state. Death on a fairytale afternoon, an afternoon of flowers and peacocks, rose-scented and breeze-washed. Agnes Morley, that was her name, dead of a bundle of Darvon. Wrong setting, but—

She thought about the Los Angeles freeways, people monotonously killed or maimed daily. And the casualty rate among her film cohorts—a suicide, and that so-called accidental shooting, a director high on heroin, finding his wife in bed with his burly new rock star.

There was nothing new about death. And no real reason to feel so personally stricken, so stunned with guilt. The thing to do was to get this drink down and let quiet and calm, and a sense of proportion and perspective, gradually flow back.

That made two people in a day and a half. But she had felt only civilized, objective, fleeting pity about the stranger, Aloysius Gorman; not this throbbing involvement with the extinction of Agnes Morley. When had the Darvon, in a silent avalanche of hopelessness, been taken? If on getting his request over the telephone, she had said to Conor, "Yes, of course," and gone over to Dunragh right away, would . . . ?

You could blow this up, tiptoe fearfully from second to second, and drive yourself stark mad.

She turned her attention to externals. A splendid pair of whippets strolled by her, one white, one black. A long-faced man at a table nearby lifted his glass and recited to it in his accent of finely honed music, "Home is the sailor, home from the sea, And the hunter home from the hill," Robert Louis Stevenson's *Requiem,* wasn't that?

From the bar, a woman's voice, English, aristocratically carrying, not giving a damn who heard what she had to say, "You know and I know that all dear Barbara's troubles stem from the fact that she's afflicted with penis envy . . ."

In the booth behind her, two men made thirsty lip-smacking sounds. Their voices a refreshment, soft and low and rippling. "I had to get out of McCane's, so noisy I couldn't hear myself spit. . . . What is that fellow Conor Niall doing here at all? I hear he's a screen star. Are they making another film?"

"No, no, he's on the news, the American news. As for why he's here, something for the tele*vision,* you can count on that."

"Well then we'd better mind our manners, hadn't we? He may have a little secret camera under his lapel to see what Leam is up to."

Was there no place where you could get away from him? But this was a small closed world which echoed and re-echoed with itself and its occupants. Especially, she supposed, the comings and goings of the handsome and probably to their eyes glamorous international Kinsellas.

Would he have heard by now, been told about the unfortunate end his protégée had come to? Or would it be her next-to-impossible task to break it to him. "That girl you were worried about,

Conor." "Yes, what about her? How is she?" "Well, as a matter
of fact, she's dead—was when I got there. For tea, you know."

The long-faced man at the next table studied her through an
inner haze of whiskey. He was a carpenter but artistically inclined.
There was a sort of flickering and dappling as expressions followed each other across the fair slender face. She's like a forest
creature, he thought, gliding in and out of sun and shadow. The
tilted eyes suggested a young deer. Pretending to be gazing past
her, out the window, he went on with his attentive musings.

She's slain for some reason.

She's not seeing this place at all, she's seeing something somewhere else.

Ah—now she's fighting back. Good girl, down with the whiskey!

She's made up her mind about something. What else would that
suddenly lifted chin, slight head turn, and widening eyes mean?

Good luck to you, my girl, whatever way you think you've
found to pull yourself up out of your hole.

Why, Sara asked herself, driving firmly back toward Leam, are
the most obvious things the ones you often don't think your way
to? They just come along and whack you over the head, all by
themselves.

Not six yet. She couldn't be expected back for a while from
Nou's no doubt lavish tea. No, Mrs. Broth reported, Fitz wasn't
with her, she had gone off alone. She added powerfully, "Gold or
no gold, he's close to twice her age and a foreigner at that—I mean
a *real* foreigner."

As she had driven herself, there seemed no sensible way of
turning up to fetch her back. But you could always be a rude
American, dropping in jovially, uninvited. "Just passing by, wondered if Sara was still here? Yes, thank you, I will take a cup of
tea."

Ten minutes' drive brought him to the white gate, closed. The
gatekeeper's house was more than obviously unoccupied; it had
been skillfully turned into a picturesque charming ruin, ivy-
covered, its walls partially removed here and there, its roof gone
but the roof corners topped with urns of flame and pink geraniums. At the right side of the gate, he spotted what must be a

house telephone in a white-painted iron niche. He picked it up and listened to a brief ringing. Then Banning, Oxfordian, came on.

Buttoned-up kind of voice the man has, Conor thought, and now even more so.

"Is Sara still there? I was passing and thought I'd stop by and see her home if she's on the point of leaving—in case of highwaymen and similar hazards along the road."

There was a short pause. In an unamused and antisocial manner, Banning said, "No, she is not here. She left some time ago."

"Oh, too bad. While I have you, how is the Morley girl? Better?"

"The mother is apparently visiting and hasn't been contacted, so I'm afraid I can't go into her condition."

Time for the rude act. "Screw that, Banning, is she or isn't she all right? She's something of a responsibility of mine, you know, I brought her to you. These fences of yours are easy to climb over."

But, with a sickening lurch under his ribcage, he knew. *"The mother hasn't been contacted."* Soldiers killed or missing in action, victims of air crashes, names withheld until the relatives were notified.

"This is unofficial," Banning began harshly, "but since as you say you brought her here instead of to her own home—she's dead. Suicide. And now I absolutely refuse to discuss it any further. You can get the details from the Garda when they're free to talk to the curious." The line went abruptly empty.

Find Sara first. If she'd been there, she'd know. Suicide? When, how, why? But if she had written poems to him, if she had loved him . . . in obscure lives, there did occur tremendous silent crashes. It was probably shock that, right now, was making him refuse to accept the simple tragic story.

He has gone, and I will go with him . . .

Find Sara.

Twelve

"Where, exactly, do you think you're going, Sara?" Conor asked, leaning against the doorframe just inside the bedroom.

She had opened the front door of the cottage to his knock just three minutes ago. Eyes staringly wide, the green going dark, she said, "You've heard?"

"Agnes? Yes. Over the house telephone at Dunragh."

He looked past her into the bedroom, at the bed heaped with clothes and the open suitcase on the creamy old crocheted bedspread.

"You'll want a report, of course." She gave it to him fast and flat. But in painful accuracy she left nothing out. When she came to Banning's half statement "I suppose the interview with the police, the disgrace—" she was interrupted.

"What disgrace?"

"I don't know. He ended up by saying he wasn't making sense."

Disgrace? Her poems? Had policemen's hands, inspecting the cottage, turned them up, to read aloud, to elbow each other in the ribs and chortle at?

Looking at the floor, Sara finished, "To tell you I'm terribly sorry I didn't go earlier would be the understatement of the year. Or my life."

He could find nothing immediately to say to this; at least nothing glib and brushing-away. She turned and went back into the bedroom and yanked open both top dresser drawers. A whirl of silk scarves flew through the air and landed on the accumulating pile.

A nineteenth-century Mahon, justly fond of her own beauty, had had the pale yellow painted walls inlaid with mirror panels all around the room. She didn't want, again, to look directly at him, into his eyes, but the room showed an almost menacing surround of him. Back here, profile there, full face beside her, arms quietly at his sides. A dozen Conors to contend with.

To his question about her packing, she answered, "To Dublin, for a conference. You've heard about conferences? And then, London for a bit, a friend of mine—oh, *hell,* why am I lying to you?" He saw reflected, repeated, the acute distress distorting her face.

He picked up from the bed a long evening dress of a pale far-mountain blue. "I've always loved you in this." He walked to the closet and put it back on a hanger.

Watching him, not at all acknowledging what he was doing, she went on in a low uncertain voice, "There are just times when you have to be away by yourself. In any case—I see no earthly reason why I have to explain my itineraries to you."

Turning again to the dresser, she pulled open the second drawer and tossed out underclothes, silk and lace and expensive synthetics, apricot and misted green and *café au lait.*

"Linen still crushes, doesn't it?" He rescued a suit of raspberry red with a kilt-pleated skirt, found a hanger with clips, and with calm quick fingers fastened the clips to the skirt's waistband. Next he replaced in the closet a Burberry raincoat and an airy black lace cocktail dress. Musingly, "Mostly new, but I recognize a few things, this dress—"

Now it was she who could find nothing to say. Except a winded, "This is ridiculous," which was saying nothing at all.

"Is it me you're running away from, Sara?" He went over to her, took a folded orange mohair shawl from her hand and put it back in the open drawer. "Or people suddenly dying to the right and left of you—is it that you're frightened?"

She turned her face a little away. He was very close.

"You? And why should I run away from you?" An attempt at pride, scorn—of what importance to her was he, to be fled from. And then she, articulate Sara, lost her way, vocally. "It's just that I can't stand—I'm all, I don't know—" Tears began running down her cheeks and she put her palms to her face. "Among other things, right now, I'm shattered right down to the soles of my feet. Leave me alone, will you?"

He cupped his hands around her shoulders, which were beginning to shake. "No, I will not leave you alone, not in this state.

You know very well, Sara, that you can pack a bag and take a plane somewhere, anywhere, and when you get there and open the bag—lying right on top will be whatever you're running away from. The very first thing you'll have to unpack . . ."

She gave up the fight against confused grief, or rather was conquered by it.

He took her weeping into his arms, at first for comfort, cheek warm and hard against hers. "We've come to an understanding that you'll stay, now haven't we." Voice soothing, close to her ear. "Of course you're shattered. So am I, Sara. So am I, darling." He kissed her gently and felt her body give something like a shiver, or a sigh of the flesh.

A tick of time, immeasurable. Back then, last year, if they had been as they were now, Conor would have taken her off to the sweet bed at any hour.

She tensed away her own softness and said, muffled against him, "The usual, I suppose, selfish human clasping in the face of somebody else's final disaster—"

With his old maddening delightful way of feathering his lips against hers as he spoke, "Do you really think so? Let's just see."

After three tries, you sink and drown. Head thrown back, she said hoarsely, almost desperately, "Let me go, Conor, you're only making it *worse—everything—*"

A swift and sudden motion behind him, an arm hooked around his neck, wrenching him powerfully backward. He made a half landing on the end of the bed on a tumble of Sara's rainbowed underclothes.

Fitz stood over him. Both his color and his silence were dangerous.

For the moment, protect Sara from him. The lick of his rage might scorch her too.

The best defense is a good attack. Defense for her, attack on her from him. He got to his feet. "I was trying to make up for raising hell with Sara. I had no idea she'd dissolve in tears like this."

"And what have you to raise hell with Sara about?" The question, words carefully spaced, of an icy stranger.

"Agnes Morley, the girl I called her about this afternoon. All right, Sara, I won't turn the knife again. We have no idea yet when she actually did die. I'm going to the Garda. You can tell the whole sad story to Fitz."

The truth, or almost the truth. There had been a few fine swift seconds when they were inseparably part of each other again.

He left behind him in the mirror-silvered room a silence that seemed to beat on the ears like a troubled heart.

Images of Fitz surrounding her now, one taut question from head to foot. She looked at the clenched threatening hands at his sides. "First of all, relax your hands, Fitz."

"They'll relax when they feel like it," he said. "Now what was this that brought you two so touchingly together?"

Wanting not to repeat it, turn the knife herself, she told him. He moved from his cool three-foot distance and as if to verify something put a finger to her wet cheek.

"And is that what all this packing was about? There are still chunks of you missing."

She saw how deeply troubled he still was and thought about putting her arms around him and showing him without any nonsense that everything was all right. Then it struck her that this would be a form of betrayal. But betrayal of whom?—herself, Fitz, or Conor?

"I'm overdue in Dublin to talk about the last three scripts. They want a change here and there. I thought I'd make a quick dash."

"Or run," Fitz said. "From I don't know what. I hope not me, Sara."

But I'm not running away, Sara said to herself, I'm bolting. There's a difference. Panting and pursued . . . or taking the bit, the initiative in your teeth and tearing off to freedom. Leaving behind the hot and cold showers of emotion, Fitz, Conor; not to mention, not to mention ever again, Agnes Morley.

She had plenty of money, friends, nothing to tie her helpless here. Places to go to she loved and missed, the gardeny house in Chelsea, in London, where she could always get her favorite three rooms, the enchanting expensive garret in Paris.

The silence was bad. Into it came an imperious barking at the front door. She went thankfully to let Vesper in. He stalked in an inquiring fashion through the cottage, as if checking her protection. Then, satisfied, he came into the bedroom and like a citadel collapsing allowed himself to lie down at her feet.

Fitz smiled without warmth. "St. Francis of Leam. Cairin's not to be pried away from here, and this one's found a second home. I suppose in a way that explains Conor."

The first thing to do was to get out of the bedroom. There was something about him, a sense of pent-up power about to loose itself on her, perhaps not in anger but in a definitive claiming.

Moving to the door, she said, "Get yourself a drink and me one too. You seem remarkably calm about that poor girl, Fitz."

"I'm not remarkably calm about anything. I hardly heard what you were saying—I had other matters on my mind." He gave his head a slight collecting shake and then said over his shoulder as he went to the kitchen, "I am indeed sorry. She was, I think, Gorman's girl. Then it isn't true, Shakespeare's disclaimer, 'Men have died and worms have eaten them, but not for love.'" How hard his voice sounded.

Coming back in with their drinks, he said, "Tomorrow's my birthday. Your scripts can wait a few days, can't they?"

When had she decided that she wasn't, after all, going to bolt? It was safer to think that the decision was being made right now.

"I suppose so, yes." She lifted her glass. "To . . ."

"Us, love," Fitz said. "Cat got your tongue? *Us.*"

Banning applied himself to the tape recorder more for his own later, calmed listening than for Nou's.

No time to think it out in his head right now, with the girl's mother and brother about to descend on the castle and claim their dead. And with details to see to, at Nou's orders, personally: The finest casket, ten dozen roses to be sent from Dunragh when the body was allowed into its casket, an offer of a handsome memorial stone preferably of Connemara marble.

"Niall's day at the Bay," mused Banning to his machine. "And that person Upshaw firing *Mary Jean* inquiries at barmen. Then Niall on the house telephone. Wanting to, what was it? protect Sara from highwaymen and other hazards along the road. A signal to me? Highwaymen translated into caravans? But the tinkers are not armed, or at least not in any conventional way. Good God, I may be wrong, dithering. It's been a bad day to say the least, but I can't say I like the looks of this or rather the sound of it. At all."

Thirteen

"I don't know where I'd gotten the idea that your car had hit her as she crossed the road, that blind curve is bad."

It struck Conor as he drove to Glasna that, Agnes Morley dead, there would be no way to prove he hadn't knocked her down in the road. Of course, Upshaw might be of some use as a witness, but he would present a doubtful one. Odd train of thought—now where had it come from? There would be an inquest. A verdict of suicide while of unsound mind (he would have, finally, to tell the attentive ears about the poems; they gave another, deeper dimension to grief and shock). And that the unfortunate demise had taken place at Dunragh Castle, after every care had been swiftly seen to—the doctor, the ambulance, the X ray—would probably quench at the source any possible question.

Question? What question? But then, why had he been obscurely worried about Agnes Morley? Why had he wanted Sara's eye on her? Wait for the answers until he had talked to the Garda.

Sergeant Dall was on the desk at the ugly little brick station house. Conor had felt at first sight of him a mild dislike which he hadn't troubled to analyze. Crinkly brown hair, round pink face, upturned nose, blue eyes too small. Mouth dainty, pink, and pursed.

"Well now, Mr. Niall, we're not talking to the press until tomorrow morning, we don't want the family bothered."

What press?

"I took her there and she was in a way my responsibility," Conor said again, generations of authority in his expression and his voice.

"Since you insist, sir, then this is strictly between us," Dall said with a put-upon sigh. "It's a sad disgraceful story—"

"To die in your twenties is a disgraceful fate, I agree."

At his tone, whip-edged, Dall flushed. "She'd sneaked over to his cottage with him barely cold and set to robbing it of anything she thought had any value. Wait a minute—"

He reached under the counter and with a ruler under one of its straps lifted out the black plastic handbag. "No, don't touch it, fingerprints. Anyway, jewelry, money, this fine old piece of silver you see sticking out. Thought she'd get away with it, but someone, some friend of Wishy's, we don't know who yet but we will—someone caught her at it and sent her running and she left it behind at his cottage."

Wrong, not true, all wrong, thudded in Conor's head as, looking at the handbag, pitiful, the maximum size and shine for the minimum money, he saw instead the pain-widened hazel eyes looking up at him in whole trust, heard the voice, "I went to get the poems I wrote to Wishy."

"We faced her with it all right, and what did she throw but a show of hysterics. Oh no, *she* wouldn't steal from Wishy, not she! Loved him, says she." He tapped the handbag with the tip of a ballpoint pen. "This stuff just walked into her purse. Just as well, what's happened—she'd have been ruined, the disgrace with her and hers all their lives."

There were questions Conor wanted to ask, must ask; but not of this man with his hostile made-up mind. However, the most obvious one spoke itself before he could contain it, "She told me she'd been struck. Suppose whoever it was faked this theft?"

"Of course she came by an injury. A hard push or shove. Someone in a fury catching her at what she was up to, it must have been face on, because it was the back of her head hit the dresser and left a blood smear. You'll notice, by the way, she named no one to us in this department. So then she just took to her heels."

Nothing more to be had here, not from censorious Dall. "Thanks for the information, or for your version of it." He had just closed the door of the station house when Dall picked up the telephone and called Dunragh Castle.

On the way home from Glasna, the evening billowing above now with plum-purple clouds holding rain, he found himself slipping into a kind of fantasy. It was Sunday, and CBS's "60 Minutes" had just ticked on, on the television screen. Whose voice was he hearing—Safer, Wallace, Rather, Reasoner? Perhaps his own.

Open on a fishing boat pulling into a pier at night. Natural sounds, water clucking, men talking, whistling, sea gulls swooping and screaming for fish guts. Voice over, narrating: "Her name is the *Mary Come Home* but her other name, shared with many such battered cheerful little boats, is the *Mary Jean,* which when you think of it has a certain similarity to the Spanish word 'marijuana.'"

In late winter, he had had an assignment covering the suspected smuggling of drugs up from Florida through inland waterways. The session had centered in the dark dripping bayous of Louisiana. He remembered a mule-drawn cart driven to a rotting little dock, great heavy burlap bags being handed up from a silently slipping boat to the man on the dock. They had, invisible, filmed it all, and of necessity acquainted the local police with the matter. The police had impounded the film—for closer examination, they said—and later innocently explained that their projector was faulty and had ripped the reel beyond repair. Bought and paid for, they were, of course—Dall's face flashed into his mind. Save Dall for a later sequence.

Mules. Donkeys, horses, caravans, like the three parked not far from the gates of Dunragh. A common sight anywhere in Ireland. People living to themselves, apart and private and free, a race within a race. Caravans rocking across the waist of Ireland from the Atlantic over to the Irish Sea, or to St. George's Channel, transferring their cargo to other—probably—fishing boats with access to the ports of Spain, France, England, and Holland.

Ireland the innocent country it was, religion-dominated still, great stretches of it empty, and the drug closest to the hearts of many of its people plainly and simply alcohol. The last place you would think of if you were bent on tracing a vein of illicit traffic.

Perhaps not just the caravans; horse vans, hay and feed carriers, dusty familiar vehicles going about their daily business in a country largely agricultural.

You had to sketch all this in a few shots, a few sentences, and get on with your story.

Brief but wrenching camera coverage of Aloysius Gorman's funeral, preferably with the rain pouring down at the graveside. "Every once in a while Wishy Gorman felt called upon to wrestle with the devil. This took the form of publicly denouncing any fellow citizen he suspected of sin or wrongdoing. Three nights before his funeral, he was going to Kilkieran Bay to read, he said, the riot act to the *Mary Jean*. He never got there. He died, sadly and suddenly. Tripped and fell and drowned in this peaceful stream, a trout fisherman's paradise when there isn't a body to be hooked."

Agnes's funeral? No, too many graves. A photograph of her if there was one, camera moving in on it. "This was Wishy Gorman's girl. Note the past tense." Camera going up the lane to the cottage and peering within. "On a sunny morning the day after Gorman's death . . ."

Agnes and her poems. Agnes hanging, bleeding, over a stone wall. Agnes at last safe in bed. And then the Garda coming to accuse her of robbing the dead Wishy. The film sequence ran vividly before his eyes. Left alone . . . desperately thinking, Holy Mother of God the disgrace of it.

(Or, write in a new scene. Hands holding a steaming cup or bowl. "Of course it tastes bitter, but it'll do you all the good in the world. Doctor Quin ordered that you have it without fail." Excise this last? Dump it? No, put it away on a shelf somewhere in case it might come in handy later, when this never-never project got its never-never final editing.)

Cut, from the bed to an exterior shot. Concentrate the lens's eye on the splendors of Dunragh. Terrific contrast, of course, to the funeral in the rain and the modest thatched cottage—those blooming rhododendron hedges, peacocks, terrace, long graceful gray-golden stone facade towered at each corner.

It would be a little too much to expect the owner to pose, smiling, on the shallow steps between the urns of roses.

Was this knee-jerk prejudice, abstract hatred, laying it all at General Loc Nou's door? His military reign in Vietnam had been one of consistent villainy, but did that put him at the head of Drugs by Caravan, Inc.? Maybe it was Banning. Maybe Nou was blissfully ignorant of the operation. Perhaps it had nothing at all to do with Dunragh.

But it didn't matter at the moment, he wasn't on the air with it, it was all in his head so far. He was only letting half-buried impressions, bits and tags of emotion and observation, rise to the surface of his consciousness and form together. To make one almost cohesive story, one ugly tragic segment, on his own imaginary "60 Minutes."

Rain splashed his face, and he stopped to put up the Morris's canvas top, a laborious manual operation. Odd. The car was now standing only a few yards away from the buttercupped bank her hair had been trailing into. With some idea of pulling himself back to right now, to reality, to seeable and touchable things, he maneuvered the car tiltingly up on the bank, off the road, locked it, and went back to the gap in the wall where the grass-centered lane led to Wishy Gorman's cottage.

The windows were lighted. That One's sister from Letterkenny? Yes, it appeared when the top half of the front door was opened to his knock. A very old, very wrinkled, ill-natured face; a voice that had obviously been waiting to pour complaints at somebody.

He identified himself and, not knowing exactly what he was wanting at the cottage or from it, asked politely, "Is there anything I can do?"

"You can come in and you can take a cup of tea and you can look at the wilderness they're after having me live in—they say the film didn't turn out and they have to come back and take some more pictures—a witch's den, that's what it is, look around you, will you."

And she a most appropriate inhabitant for the witch's den, in long dusty black, coal-dark eyes in enormous hollowed pits, thin gray hair skewered at the top of her head into a meager knot.

"They" being he supposed the Garda, having to retake photographs of the scene. "They said they'd be here at four and look at it after six now and all the people coming here tomorrow to be watered and whiskied and fed, and when am I to clean it up? Am I expected to spend the night at it?"

Making sympathetic noises, he took a cup of near-black tea from her hand. At this strength, it gave almost as feelable a physical lift as strong drink.

He cast a quick eye over the toppled newspapers, the wrenched-out drawers, the heap of bedding, sheets, blanket, clean old faded comforter, on the earth floor. There was a piece of clear plastic taped loosely over the corner of the dresser, the place where she had supposedly hit her head when knocked backward by whoever had discovered her at her secret stealing.

But—he almost said it aloud—*women don't search this way*. They probe and pry, delicately, carefully. They are deep in their bones house creatures no matter how distantly removed from menial tasks. They cover their tracks.

Only half hearing the aunt working her way through an interminable list of grievances, he found himself sketching another sequence. Someone in the cottage when Agnes got there, someone swiftly and roughly searching. Then her timid entry. He mustn't be seen and recognized by her. From behind, a quick blow on the back of the head, and while she lay motionless a hurried stuffing of her handbag with whatever he could lay hands on. Easy enough, with hurried fingers, to dabble her blood on the dresser.

"—and the will was caught in a corner of the drawer and was all but torn in half, and money stolen, the Garda said, God knows was it the sum and total of all he had—"

Sergeant Grady appeared in the open top half of the door, camera strap over his shoulder. Once inside, he poured kindly oil. Here was the money from the handbag, Mrs. O'Dea, forty-seven pounds. And yes, Wishy did have money in the bank, he didn't want to say exactly how much in front of—giving Conor an amiable glance—but his wife's brother was the assistant manager and said it was a nice little sum. And he'd be out of here in ten minutes flat and she could get to her tidying up. It was a good thing to have work to occupy your hands when—

Conor set down his cup, having got what he hadn't known, coming here, he wanted. Grady said to him, "You wouldn't hardly credit it, would you, sir? Two of them in a bit over twenty-four hours. God's a mysterious fellow, isn't he?"

"He is indeed," Conor said.

God?

He thought he would like to talk to Grady, but not now, not here.

I won't, James vowed when he rose from his waking nap, let that man out of my sight, no matter what, from now on. I will not let him hector or corner Bel. I will not let him, ever again, be alone with her.

He toyed with the idea of driving Upshaw some immense distance away, asking him to get out of the car on some pretext—

perhaps to check a tire—and then speeding off and abandoning him far from any transport. But he had been ordered by his doctor not even to consider driving a car.

Call the hay and grain people, offer them a bribe to summon Upshaw right away to his new job? A hundred pounds? No, they'd think such an obviously strong desire to get rid of a relative's presence might make their proposed new employee a questionable choice. The man's whole future might be blighted.

Get in touch with her sisters? Ivy, living in the South of France, would be of no immediate use. Beatrice, near enough, in Dublin. But Beatrice terrified him, and besides if Bel had wanted her ear, she knew where to find it.

Tell Fitz? Tell him *what?* "Upshaw's a good deal more than a nuisance to your mother. Can't you get rid of him?" Fitz, bound up as he was with Sara Parry and his horses; Fitz gazing at him, puzzled, and saying, "It's her house, James. Certainly it's up to her whether he stays or goes."

He wouldn't have been the first nuisance Bel had taken in. There was another remote cousin, Hypatia, in a daze of sherry from morning till night; she had stayed three months. And an old friend of Paul's father, Valentine something, who wanted peace and quiet in which to write his memoirs, and whom James in all his charity considered certifiably mad. Valentine, five months.

But neither of them at any time during their residencies had gone over Bel like a drowning wave.

He drank his tea by himself. The cleaning tornado had repaired to the butler's pantry where every piece of china and crystal was ordered to be taken down and washed, and God have mercy, said Mrs. Broth, on any of you who chips—breakage not even to be thought of.

Ripple and quivers of reflected light from the water swam over the white walls and ceiling. A scent of cooking strawberries floated in from the distant kitchen; Mrs. Broth's preserve under way. The drawing room, immaculate and smelling of wax, every pillow puffed, fresh fire burning, should have been peaceful, but it wasn't.

A rodent is loose in this house, thought James, with the plague in its cornered, swift bite. Even when he's away, Upshaw, there is still the sense of the rodent, behind a door or flashing horribly down the stairway.

He got up to look at the mail in the poppy-painted glass basket on the hall table. Copious, most of it for Fitz, nothing for Upshaw. What if it was an invention, the check—what if he stayed forever?

There were a dozen matters in the gardens and greenhouse wanting his attention, but he sat on, as the sky began to darken, and waited.

Finally, feet on the stairway—Upshaw's light and, to James's mind, furtive tread. He gave him several seconds and then followed quietly, to see if it was his own room or bathroom he was heading for.

At the top of the stairs, he was just in time to see Bel's bedroom door closing. Feeling a faint tremor of rage and tension running through his body, he went close to listen, and if necessary to help.

Upshaw hadn't knocked, but had silently turned the knob and slipped in. Bel was in a half doze on her bed, a condition she recognized as a craven retreat. She turned her head sharply and swung her feet to the floor.

"I've had all but enough of the hospitality of this house," Upshaw said, the words the uglier because of the sibilant softness of them. "You have exactly twenty-four hours, which I call generous. That's your deadline, Mrs. K."

The door was pushed open. James stood just outside. Very pale, he demanded, "Deadline for what?"

Let everything collapse? Let the skies fall? Or make an effort?

Nearly, in her weariness, impossible, but she managed, "It's nothing of any importance, James. But it's a sort of private thing . . . a secret. Not mine, but . . . but, John's."

"Everybody's," Upshaw said with new-found bullying confidence, turning to go. "Unless."

Fourteen

Bel went to the window to put her face together again. A drift of sweetness lifted the hair at her temples. The limes. Thank God for the life-reminding limes.

She was aware of the presence of James, still in the room. James silent, giving her time.

After several minutes, "I won't pry," James said very quietly. "But can I help?"

She turned to him, hoping her features were arranged as they should be. *Could* he help?

All her personal references, decorum, propriety, were floating off somewhere, no color, no black and white, just gray. James's thin generous hand reaching out to her—it might be all right in last-minute desperation to accept, figuratively, one finger of it.

Without giving herself time to think, to draw back, she said, "Yes, James, you can. A *very* small Pandora's box, and it ought to be closed again by the end of the day. If you can think of some way to incarcerate him about . . ." One hundred and fifty miles, three hours, Dublin with luck at eleven. "About eight in the morning, until I get safely off. And if he asks, tell him I'll be back without fail sometime in the evening."

"I'm sure I can manage one way or another," said James, never noted for his efficiency except with his flowers. "In the meantime, I am going to take you away from this house. I don't think it's good for you. We'll go to the Queen of Corrib and drink, and have something to eat, and you do not have to say one word."

"All right, I'd like to." Frightful company she would be, but she could try her old game of looking away again, trying to concentrate her being on something else, something pleasant or promising.

It didn't work.

There was a thriving trade at the Queen tonight, which ought to have been all to the good. Voices, laughter. Radio music, the waltz from *Der Rosenkavalier*. Eugene Ormandy and the Philadelphia Orchestra, James's ear noted. People passing their candle-lit booth, Bel, how are you? Darling, how nice. And James, are you romping then? Who's to see to your freesias? Do have a drink with us—oh, in a hurry? Then next time, or perhaps tomorrow, the birthday . . .

Over their whiskey, James tried to bring her back from wherever she was. "These people have a special talent for cineraria," he said. "Though I must say I do not care for the pink."

He got a murmur that might connote anything. Don't, he thought, talk about that poor girl Agnes Morley. Don't, under any circumstances, tell a woman on the brink about another who has gone fatally over it.

Wanting to get through the remoteness, he said something he'd meant to keep to himself.

"Conor's in love with Sara, did you know that?"

Dazed glance finally meeting his; then a sharp blink. "How on earth did you arrive at that conclusion?"

"You've only to look at him looking at her." James swirled the liquid in his glass. "And the air around them . . ."

"Do you mean *she's* in love with *him* too? But they've only just—"

"They both come from another country, Bel. They may have been quite good friends there."

"Oh dear. Oh, poor Fitz. But perhaps they mayn't . . ."

There she went, sliding away again, losing Conor and Sara and Fitz in her own mists.

The emeralds, five, six, seven thousand? *What if they were fake?* She would never have known; she had taken them on trust. Because Paul, her husband Paul, had said they were emeralds. She put a hand to her throat.

"Do you need air? If you'll let me get past you to the window—"

"No, I'm fine." No, I'm just feeling for a necklace I'm not wearing, running the possible liars of green stones through my fingers, James.

He'd hardly told her the exact truth on that long-ago night in their bedroom. Or had he?

She had said to him that it was kind of Amy Veagh to leave money to him and then aloud wondered why. He had said that he could only imagine that she had no one else in the world.

James began his vigil in the third-floor hall at seven thirty. To lend authenticity, he still wore his pajamas and slippers and warm dark blue wool robe. His meditations yesterday afternoon on the nature of Upshaw's presence in the house had given him the idea.

If it didn't work, if the bathroom report didn't scare off Upshaw, he had an alternative plan. Take him along to his own room on the second floor, say that it was only fair that Upshaw have some memento of their, probably, great-grandfather in common. Get out the leather box with the cuff links and evening studs, the rings, the priceless old watch with its gold chain. Even before breakfast, pure greed ought to absorb Upshaw for a time. He would no doubt sum up his cousin by marriage, James, as a doddering idiot, giving away jewelry at this unlikely hour, but that was all right. However, try the bathroom first.

At a quarter of eight, the maid's room door was cautiously opened. Upshaw, barefoot, in his trousers and sleeved undershirt which had a grayish hue.

James took the flat of his palm from the bathroom door. "I don't suppose he can get out, but—" He tried the knob nervously.

"Who can get out?"

Making himself sound breathless, James said, "The bath on the floor below is in use, and I thought I'd pop up here. Just when I reached the top of the stairs I saw an immense, oh ghastly, *rat* scuttle in. The door was a little ajar—if there's anything I hate more than a rat, it's a terrified rat waiting to spring. Perhaps you mightn't mind going in first just to see if after all he'd hide behind a towel or something and not attack?"

"No thank you," Upshaw said in obvious horror.

"Well, I didn't think so. I thought I'd wait a few minutes here to warn you. And to take you down to our third bathroom, I didn't know if you knew where to find it. Good God, was that a squeak? But of course he can't get out, they can't work knobs, can they? I must get one of the stable boys to come up here with a shovel."

"Wait till I put my shirt and shoes on. I appreciate the guard duty. I was bitten by a rat when I was a kid. I'll never forget it."

As they passed Bel's door, James gave it a light prearranged tap. Upshaw followed him trustingly across the hall, through the dining room and butler's pantry and kitchen to the stone staircase to the cellars. Mrs. Broth, at the stove frying bacon, gave them an interested glance.

James had the key in his bathrobe pocket, and he had oiled the lock last night. A key probably hadn't been turned in it for decades.

"You go first. There are shaving things and I hope clean towels, no bath I'm afraid but a good needle shower." He opened the door to the gymnasium-fitted room. Outer walls of stone, and the door itself was thick, in case Upshaw began shouting. Not that anyone in the house would be in a great hurry to come to his aid.

The key worked with reassuring silence. James looked at his watch and decided he deserved a cigarette while he continued his guard duty.

Upshaw took his time. He was still a guest in this house. He showered and shaved, and while doing so tried to reckon up the cost of all the expensive exercising equipment gathering dust. Money here, there, and everywhere, and he still waiting with his empty hand out!

Well, he'd told her. He'd given the screw a good sharp turn. Twenty-four hours . . . his mind immediately masking out the appalling source of these figures, this time span.

Yes, a good sharp squeezing unanswerable turn. She hadn't said no. But then how could she?

It was a quarter past eight when he got his clothes back on. James saw the knob turn and again silently unlocked the door and held it closed for a few seconds.

"It sticks," he said. "Ah, much refreshed I see."

"Yes. Sorry to have kept you waiting all this time."

"That's perfectly all right," said James.

Bel was a good driver, fast, confident, and bold. She took her dark green Jaguar two-seater and when a stretch of empty road opened up let it hurtle. The feeling of being in command of danger rather than subject to it was for a time a release.

Be careful, though. It didn't particularly matter if anything happened to her, but there were dogs to be considered, sheep, chickens, children, not yet borne down by a weight of hopelessness.

In her haste and fear of being caught by Upshaw while escaping, in spite of James's cautions and schemes, she had forgotten her umbrella, and the cold rain was starting.

In her bedroom at seven thirty he had said, "Can't I go with you, Bel?"

"No. I'm alone."

She didn't mark her words, but he did. How strange. What a sad mysterious slip. Not, I must go alone—"I'm alone."

Upshaw, when he demanded to know where she was, as of course he would, was to be told she had gone off to Dublin on business. "And remember, James, back this evening *absolutely* without fail."

The furs were in a suitcase in the boot, smuggled out late last night so no one would ask where she was going with her suitcase. Her jewelry was in one section of the triple-pouched Hermès handbag Conor had sent her for her birthday. Not just the necklace. She'd scrambled everything in after all.

One hundred and fifty miles could seem a relatively short distance when you were on your way to friends or festivities and had someone with you you could talk to, and could spare attention and delight for the soft surprises of the landscape. Or it could seem endless, alone, in the rain.

She left the Jaguar in a parking garage near St. Stephen's Green. Before getting out of it she gave a brief uncaring glance at herself in the driving mirror and was shocked at the white and suddenly elderly woman who looked blankly back at her. Wisps of blown hair plastered to her forehead, mouth a little open, corners turned down, as if to utter a cry. Couldn't look like a madwoman when she walked into the jewelers'. She got out her comb and lipstick, tidied what could be tidied—not the expression of the face itself, nothing to be done about that. On the rear-window ledge she found a black felt hat with a broad droopy brim which would offer some kind of concealment for its distressed, its lost, wearer.

Dalming and Corney was only a block or so away from the Green. Don't worry about an umbrella now, buy one when she'd finished with her transaction. Please God let none of her friends turn up. "Bel, what are you doing in Dublin, how marvelous!"

No need to feel furtive as well as lost. Paul had given her the necklace and now she was in a way giving it back to him. It was as simple as that.

The jewelers' was all soft gray inside, carpet, marble, painted paneled walls. A single customer, a woman in burly tweeds, sat on a gilded chair in front of a glass-enclosed counter and gazed at a ring on one fat upheld finger. The shop attendant, in morning dress, reached behind him to press a button and another morning dress appeared from an archway at the back of the shop. A young man, handsome, with a soft voice.

Through stiff lips, Bel murmured, "I'm here to sell, not to buy."

"Then we'll want to be by ourselves, won't we. Follow me, madame." They went into a large booth hidden discreetly behind gray velvet curtains, where secrets could be shown, secrets could be bought and sold.

Probably every woman's hand shook at a time like this? She got out two fistfuls from her bag and dumped them on the gray velvet tabletop. The attendant, upon whose slender golden tiepin was engraved "Mr. Minott," arranged the necklace and her other odds and ends as though for display.

Seated, because her legs would no longer hold her, she watched him studying an emerald through his loupe. Then he laid the necklace down and gave her a long examining if polite look. Of course, she thought. How does he know I didn't steal it, how does he know I'm not a crook?

"It's your own," she said, hating the supplicating eagerness of her voice. "I mean, it came from here. I remember the box . . . ivory leather . . . I assume there'll be a bill of sale somewhere? Kinsella, Paul Kinsella, and I have identification with me, I'm Mrs. Kinsella."

Looking at the underside of the clasp, he found the tiny Dalming and Corney hallmark, the two initials intertwined. This seemed to unlock his enthusiasm and admiration.

"Very fine, Mrs. Kinsella, very fine indeed, the stones. In a matter of this magnitude—we're talking thousands—you will have to see Mr. Dalming. Mr. Corney as you may or may not know passed away recently, a great loss."

"How many thousands?" Bel asked desperately.

"Well now, that I couldn't specify. Unfortunately, Mr. Dalming is indisposed."

Oh no.

Had she said it aloud?

"We expect him to be back at our helm no later than a week from today. In the meantime, would you like to leave these in our safe? It doesn't do, you know, to walk around with valuables on your person."

"But I must settle the sale of them today." Frantic now. Stop it.

"That is of course your affair, Mrs. Kinsella." Kindly disapproval. "I am sorry. If you change your mind, we shall hope to look forward to seeing you again today week."

She stood indecisively outside, brushed rain from her cheek, discovered she'd left her gloves in the curtained booth and went back in for them.

The furriers next? Or try another jeweler, the one on Dame Street? If they wanted proof she owned the emeralds, they could call Dalming and Corney, couldn't they?

A *laissez faire* wretchedness held her as if chained to the sidewalk. The Dame Street people mightn't handle transactions involving so much money; she seemed to remember a certain shabbiness about the place. Well, then, the furrier, but even if they bought everything it would be nowhere near—

A sudden savage pull at her shoulder sent her staggering sideways. She fell on one knee while instinctively she grasped the shoulder strap of her bag. A grimed face close, another unsuccessful tug, a whispered expletive, and then the boy—he looked to be about sixteen—turned and ran and lost himself among the Grafton Street shoppers. A man helped her to her feet, remarked that the sidewalks were indeed slippery with the rain, asked her if she was all right, and then went his way.

Her knee was skinned and bleeding through the torn nylon. In shock and pain she thought, one more pull and it would all have been gone, *everything.*

There was a sudden soft pop as a black umbrella sprang up over her head. Walter Tierne said, "Be my guest. I was just next door buying myself a tie. This morning's choice turned out in broad daylight to recollect a soft-boiled egg. *Bel,* my God, what is it?"

The sheer physical undoing of sympathy and love, near and unexpected when you have almost reached some kind of end brought tears pouring.

"I thought you were in Brussels. I needed you. Kate said—"

He gave her a large handkerchief and talked to cover the choking, gasping sounds, the wiping of her eyes and the shivering attempt to stop crying, crying right here on the street. "I came home earlier than I expected to, stalemate, a meeting scheduled now for September, patent laws cannot be hurried on their way."

His hand on her forearm was firm. "Come along with me, it's a bit early for lunch but you need haven." He looked down and saw the trickle of blood to her ankle. "Somewhere where we can talk." He hailed a taxi, although it was only a matter of minutes to the restaurant, Christie's, a favorite Kinsella haunt. Warm and quiet, pleasantly dark between pools of apricot-rose light, heavy white damask tablecloths, potted palms, pale blue and buff finches in a crystal cage near the door.

They were conducted to a corner table half concealed by the palms, obviously Walter Tierne's table whenever he wanted it. "Two, yes I think martinis," Walter said to the waiter. "No hurry about ordering, we've talking to do, Joe." And to Bel, "You'll want to tidy, you know the way."

He was Paul's oldest and closest friend as well as his partner; a large-chested, firmly stout man with merry hazel eyes, the thick black brows in startling contrast to the glistening creamy hair and fresh tight rosy skin.

Returning to him, she felt as if she had come in out of the night and the cold to a crackling hearth.

She tasted her drink, found its strength steadying, and with a directness she thought she had lost somewhere by the wayside said, "I'm in terrible trouble, Walter."

"I can see that. I'd want to have a word or so to whoever's done this to you, Bel. But go on."

"First, can you lend me ten thousand pounds? Right away? And just between the two of us? You'll get it back one way or another, I promise."

"Yes, I can, and will. Now don't go fainting on me, dear woman. Have another good swallow, do."

He waited patiently for a few moments and then said, "But that's the last paragraph of the story, Bel, what's the first?"

If he found out she intended to pay blackmail with his money, he might turn all legal and withdraw his generosity, put it back in his pocket.

"I can't right now tell you all of it." Her mind running up corridors, finding one closed door after another. Perhaps here was a door that might open; although it felt foul to look into his eyes and lie. "Relatives of Amy Veagh—you remember Amy Veagh?— people from the United States, after all this time, suddenly feel there was a frightful injustice done when she cut them out of her will and left everything to Paul, so . . ."

"Have they been at you personally?"

"No, through a representative . . . and I thought it would be only fair to . . ."

"One, it's a good thing you're not your own lawyer, Bel. And two, I never saw you in such a state about mere money. That's not really the trouble, is it."

She looked to him as she had looked the morning of Paul's funeral: as though now again she was suffering with all her soul a fresh and thunderous death. He had known her for over three decades. He could read her with an accuracy occasionally alarming. Something, he thought, about the sound of her voice, hesitant, then gathering bravery, as she said the name "Amy Veagh." As though her lips could barely force themselves to shape the three syllables.

He ordered another drink for both of them and then bent forward, hands clasped on the gleaming tablecloth. Not wanting to meet his eyes, she looked at the strong pink hands and the pattern of the damask, bunches of lilies of the valley tied with floating ribbons.

"Except for a matter of blood and parentage, I was and am Paul's brother," Walter said. "There's almost nothing about him I don't know. I know even things you don't, and now I think the time has come to tell you one of them."

Oh don't, Bel almost whispered aloud in panic. I know it, I

know it, I can't bear to hear it from still another person, however dear he is.

"Once upon a time he did a very kind and very reckless thing, but kindness doesn't always measure consequences. Amy Veagh was dying and wanted a few days of his company—no more, no less, than his presence. No lovers' reunion, no embraces renewed, just he, taking tea with her by the fire. He didn't tell you because he thought it would upset you. I wouldn't have told Kate either, but then I wouldn't have gone at all because I'm not that much a man of heart."

He was watching her face with wonder.

"Shortly after he got back from—where was it? London—he found she'd gone quite suddenly and left him pretty well everything. He was horrified. He came to me about it, wanted to refuse it, and I pointed out that it *was,* literally, her will, her wish, and that he had no right to manipulate her intentions after her death. You know and I know that it requires a good deal more generosity to take than to give. It was a sort of final statement to him, and he couldn't throw it back at her with a polite no-thank-you."

He thought that what had happened to the woman across the table from him was almost a miracle. Gradually, the drooping shoulders had begun straightening. The grayed skin, stretched too tightly, took on an inner ivory glow. The eyes, dark and stony, fixed, were flooded with brilliant violet light. Even the eyebrows seemed to change shape, springing back to their spirited arch.

Dot the last i. It shouldn't be necessary, but God only knew what version of hell this woman had been through.

"I don't want to tread on your grass, Bel, but we both know he adored you right up to the last."

Her joy, which had been gathering slowly, hung in the air about him like a cloud of scent.

Embarrassed, getting this deep into someone's privacy and pain and light-flooded release from it, he moved to practical concerns.

"Are these people accusing him, or you, of some impropriety in the matter of the estate?"

She hardly heard him. She wanted to stay for a while in her lovely fresh sunlit peace.

"Come back, come back, dear Bel. Is the ten thousand to shut them up? But now you see there's nothing to shut them up about."

I'd gladly give the man the money, Bel thought, if it's bought me this. It was half a second later that she remembered he was the one who had started the cancer.

"I suppose in a way it was," she said airily. And then to put a more seemly face on it, not look not only like a fool but a treacherous one, ready to believe anything however dreadful about Paul, "It seemed only fair, and off and on we have plenty of money."

"If you play Lady Bountiful and give it to them, the completely groundless question that's been bothering *you* may still be raised in a mind here and there."

"And if I don't and they make noises, go to law, the question will also be raised in a mind here and there. People tend to believe accusations more than denials."

"Who's this representative anyway? Send him to me, I'll deal with him."

"His name is John Upshaw." She dropped any pretense of playing Lady Bountiful. "I don't think I can do that, Walter. He'll suspect I'm sending him into some kind of trap—police, arrest."

"And your wanting the money right away—he's set up some kind of deadline?"

"The end of the day today."

"We will lunch," Walter said. "And then you are to come back with me and rest and recover yourself while I deal with a few things. Following which, we will take ourselves off to Leam. I assume you can put up an overnight guest?"

Fifteen

"Dear Mrs. Broth," said the cablegram, "we are most anxious and eager to secure your services at the earliest possible moment, and on a permanent basis. Salary fifteen thousand pounds per annum. Suite of three rooms with bath, air conditioning, private garden balcony when at home. Comparable accommodations in Rio de Janeiro, Brazil. Palm Springs, U.S.A. Paris, France. Cap Ferrat, France. New York, U.S.A. Private medical, dental, and fully paid hospital service for life. Annual bonus. Trained kitchen staff awaiting your orders. [Signed] Ali Kalid, secretary to the Honorable Mr. Hafar Mamood. Reply cable collect to the following address."

"Not bad news, I hope?" Conor asked with the liveliest curiosity. Mrs. Broth, at the stove, held the cablegram in one hand and a large spoon in the other. She was dressed for church, for Wishy Gorman's funeral, in sober brown, with a large feathered brown hat that looked like an upside-down stewpot on her billowing red hair.

"Nobody would spend this much money for a joke," Mrs. Broth said to the stove. "Or would they? Dear God, your friend's oyster cake is burning. I'll have to—"

In a confused clumsy way she scooped off the smoking batter, and dipped out another large spoonful. From his seat at the kitchen table, Ike Mendelssohn studied with interest aspects of Irish home life new to him. Cablegrams to cooks. Just before the cablegram, a case of champagne delivered, Dom Perignon. "Talk about the weight of the world," complained the delivery man. "Mrs. Fallon didn't have a card handy, but said to say it's for Mr. Kinsella's birthday, and many happy returns to him." Tucked in between the salt and pepper on the table, a large black-bound rib-boned Missal at the ready, for the funeral service. The immense

Vesper taking faintly growling exception to an open black umbrella left cocked on the floor to dry. The powerful bloody mary
in his hand just mixed for him by Conor because he had had a late
hard-drinking night. "I'll join you," Conor said. "It may be a long
day."

Ike had called him at eight last night, from Armagh in the
north. With a man named Evers, he had been covering a savage
flare-up in Belfast, the concentrated fury of which had lasted three
days. "Evers is off home. He said as long as I'd still got the Telefis
Eirann truck I might check with you to see if we're wanted yet.
My God, have you ever seen a batch of school kids set fire to a
knitting mill? Shot, they don't look good."

He and Conor had worked together before and got along
affably. "Yes," Conor said, "come on down," and gave him directions. Ike had arrived half an hour ago, leaving the Telefis Eirann
van in the drive outside the garage. He had dropped his Irish
driver at McCane's bar.

Ike had once said mournfully, "You can copyright yourself any
time you like. I can't. I come by the thousands." He was lavender-
shaved, tall, and loosely stooping. He had large knowing dark eyes
under drooped ivory lids and a fleshy mouth, the lower lip dangling as though in perpetual inquiry.

"Sorry, but you're just in time for another dead body," had
been Conor's greeting to him. "Although properly encased. After
you refresh yourself we're going to a funeral."

Nothing ever seemed to surprise Ike, but he said, "I thought
you were doing a job on the joys of drink in Irish pubs. Are we
trying to point up some sort of moral, starting off with the grave-
yard?"

"No. It's by way of being a kind of, on the side, documentary.
But in the course of duty we'll land in a pub or so."

He had thought a good deal about it the night before, lying
awake and listening for the sound of Fitz's footsteps in the hall,
Fitz's bedroom door closing.

Tuck yourself up, Fitz, and leave my girl alone.

He could, of course, go to the authorities with his bits and
scraps and guesses and theories. "There's something going on in
and around Leam that it might pay you to look into." But he had
a great mistrust of officialdom; his memories of the bought police

force in Louisiana were vivid. Dall had to him the same smell: paid for, owned, and thoroughly loyal in his disloyalty.

He thought the circumstances of the two deaths could never be proved. Wishy: A crushing blow on the head with a hand-held rock, and the disastrous unconscious submersion in water would produce—and probably had—the identical effect of a heavy fall and a self-inflicted wound in the course of it. Agnes Morley: How would it ever be known whether she had seized blindly upon the Darvon in a great sudden wave of grief and shame, or whether the fatal dose had been deliberately administered to her? The man, or woman, with the bitter medicine might not even know it was lethal, but could be following Nou-Banning directions. Whoever had given the orders would certainly not encircle the sickbed with witnesses.

And they weren't, the two of them, people of any importance. A grocery clerk who answered on occasion a mysterious moon-pull of religious fanaticism. A raw-boned girl, a maid in the employ of the man who was to all intents and purposes the local lord; a benefactor and embellishment of the town of Leam, a man who owned a castle.

The camera, to some, could be a fearsome forever recording thing. Men escorted by the police, hiding their faces with a newspaper, a hat, a hand, a fumblingly upturned coat collar. Don't look at me, don't *look* at me.

Just before he fell asleep, he remembered a summer day when he was eight. Scaling a little cliff in the woods, he had at the top come upon a great round silent writhe of sleeping blacksnakes. Before being snatched away by his mother, he had poked the snakes with a stick to see what would happen.

Mrs. O'Dea offered no objections to his filming Wishy's funeral when he drove over to see her before Ike's arrival. In fact, as he had expected, she was pleased and produced on her old thin face something resembling a beam. She signed an informal hand-written release and was promised in due time large still photographs taken from the film, suitable for framing. In color? Yes, in color. "I brought two hats with me, will you wait while you see which will look better in the picture?"

She had wanted, she said, a Solemn High Mass, but seeing as

poor Wishy might possibly have been in liquor, and it wasn't the most dignified death he could die, she settled, on second thought, for Low.

"Easier on you," Conor agreed. "Only half as long."

The funeral mass was at ten thirty. From the house, only Conor and Mrs. Broth attended, in their several ways. Upshaw was tempted to go along, just for the company. He found himself nervous and at loose ends.

When he encountered James shaved, brushed and clothed, he asked, "Where's Mrs. K.? Her bedroom door was open, the room's empty."

"Dublin for the day, on business," James said.

"Did she leave any message for me?"

"Only that she'd be back this evening. Without fail." James tried to keep the ice out of his voice. Gone for what? Back *with* what?

Well, Upshaw consoled himself, a logical development probably. Wanting money in a hurry, and lots of it, she mightn't like to go to the bank in Leam and cause talk. And maybe the Kinsellas didn't keep a large sum there.

"Was she—she didn't have sports clothes on, did she?" He was still haunted by the picture of her slipping out to sea on a boat called the *Mary Jean*.

James said no and went to close himself up in the library to worry all alone.

Ike Mendelssohn did not attend the mass but was well occupied filming from inside the van the mourners as they ascended the steps of the church in the rain. It seemed to him that most of the town had turned out. Conor, feeling that in this case a little knowledge was literally a dangerous thing, had merely told him he wanted the flesh and bones of a wet Irish funeral. They understood each other; Ike knew what to do with his camera.

To Conor's great relief and pleasure, Calvin Banning was there representing Dunragh Castle. Tall and visually mournful in a suit of great tailoring authority, the darkest of gray; white shirt, steel-gray silk tie, caped black raincoat over his arm. He took a place in a pew at about the exact center of the church: neither to be identified with family or close friends up front, or with the either sympathetic or curious other people of Leam, who tended to sit toward the back.

After mass, which was brought off in good time to accommodate a wedding immediately following, the line of cars proceeded slowly to the cemetery, a relatively new one on the edge of the town as the original half acre was well filled. At the rear was the Telefis Eirann van. Necks were craned, when it was seen parked outside the church. Hair was patted into place, ties straightened, a muddy shoe surreptitiously wiped. "They want it for the tele*vision*," Mrs. O'Dea had proudly explained to Mrs. McCane, and the word sped whispered from pew to pew.

Ike on instructions made no attempt whatever to conceal his presence and his function at the cemetery. He did keep a respectful distance from the graveside, using a zoom lens whenever he wanted, or Conor at his side requested, a closeup of a particular face; but the cables and the camera on its trolley were out in the open.

Conor had been afraid that Banning would feel his presence at the church was tribute enough from on high; but perhaps aware that he was a distinguished decoration for an obscure funeral, he continued to the grave.

Or was he there as a listener, to any theorizing mutters about the sad sudden death of poor Wishy?

After the final verses of blessing, the drift and straggle away began. People pausing, making little knots among the brash new stones to comfort themselves and each other.

Banning, with a pat on Mrs. O'Dea's shoulder, turned and walked toward the van. "Don't stop," Conor said to Ike. "Not until he's close enough for an eyelash count."

When he was two feet away and well able to assess the busy red light on the camera, he was momentarily ignored. Conor called over his shoulder, voice raised.

"Sergeant Grady! Would you mind waiting a bit, I want a word with you." Grady, out of uniform, dark blue-suited, had been at the mass too. He nodded yes, and went on talking to Father Fenn.

"*What,*" began Banning, face narrowing with rage, "incredible impossible crudity are you up to, Niall?"

"A modest little documentary," Conor explained. "Not much plot to it, more a matter of vignettes." He took from his trench coat pocket an envelope with scribbles on the back and studied it. "Next stop Kilkieran Bay, Ike, we've pretty well finished up here. With luck, we ought to find the *Mary Jean* in." And then with the air of one absorbed in work recalled to the immediate present, "Oh, while you're here, I suppose there'd be no problem in getting a permit to shoot Dunragh? The contrast, you know. Plain people and fancy. Exterior views will do nicely, although perhaps the great staircase—"

"Out of the question," Banning said. "You can indecently crash your way into the privacy of the helpless, but that's where it begins and ends." He turned and strode away. "Get that staunch back view," Conor murmured to Ike. "Quick—pairing up with that outsize angel."

He walked around a small sad child's grave to Sergeant Grady, who had just exchanged a farewell handshake with the priest. When he had tried to reach him last night, he hadn't been at the station and there was no answer at his house.

Grady, not a man inclined to keep himself to himself, had come to accept Conor as something in the nature of a colleague. After all, he had been close to the scenes of both deaths, involved by ear in the happening of one, and by car in the lead-up to the other. He was open and generous with his answers to swift questions.

If Agnes had been given tea or broth or any sustenance, the dishes had been taken away and washed. There was no sign of them in the bedroom. The plastic tube of Darvon, on its side, top off, more capsules spilled out, had lain on the edge of the bathroom sink. There was a water glass in the holder ring with her fingerprints clearly on it.

(Something like, "And did it taste that terrible? A glass of water ought to help. Here, drink it down." Conor mentally looked at the glass, perhaps loosely held in a palm on which a washcloth had been folded. Or a towel in case she showed signs of throwing up?)

"Who was attending to her? Giving her medicine, if any? Checking up to see if she was all right?"

"I suppose someone on the General's staff, or maybe Mr. Banning—if anyone. No medication was prescribed by Quin, and his orders were that she be left to sleep in peace, the longer the better."

"And who did the Darvon belong to?"

"Nou's valet. I can't this minute bring his name to my tongue, a Vietnam fellow. He has the room on the other side of the bathroom."

Grady hesitated, looking unhappy, and added, "I can't figure it at all. The main support of the mother, she was. The brother's unreliable. A very good girl in every way possible if you know what I mean. But then, she was in bad shape when we left her. Crying. I'd like to think she just wanted those things of Wishy's as keepsakes, but . . ." He shook his head in wonderment at the complexities of human nature.

Yes, they had found her poems, tucked into an old copy of *The Imitation of Christ*. They had given them to Mrs. O'Dea, and it was Grady's impression that she had burned them in the fire.

Any notes, jottings, paper reminders for his little religious crusades? Names, places, facts written down to refresh Wishy's memory? Anything, particularly, concerning Kilkieran Bay, or Ilch, or (carefully casual afterthought) a boat, the *Mary Jean?*

"No, nothing of that nature, sir." And no, not on the body, in the pockets of the soaked clothing, nothing of that kind, Mr. Niall.

Conor was given a reminder that he was expected at the inquest on Agnes Morley tomorrow at eleven. It had been planned for this afternoon, but the coroner, Grady said, was off his feed, the man a martyr to gastric troubles.

"Then as far as the Garda is concerned, Agnes Morley is a matter of, well, that's that?"

Grady gave him a troubled, puzzled look. "Yes—unless anybody gives us a reason to believe that that *isn't* that."

Upshaw was playing a game of solitaire in the drawing room when at eleven thirty the telephone in Bel's sitting room rang. He waited as to the manner born for Mrs. Broth to pick it up in the kitchen, but it just went on ringing. Cautiously, he crossed the hall and went in and answered it.

Calvin Banning said, "Ah. Lucky to have caught you at home. It's my understanding that you're only here for a short stay, and late as the invitation is I'd like to give you a spot of lunch. Must do something to brighten up funeral days, mustn't we?"

The pre-Leam Upshaw would have been flabbergasted. The

new Upshaw, almost believing that he had ten thousand pounds safely in his pocket, that he was or would be a man of substance and—keep it under your hat, but a pretty clever fellow into the bargain—was startled and then pleased. Why not? It would help pass the day.

"Yes, that's very kind of you. I'd like to. What time?"

"Say twelve thirty, a bit early, but I for one am peckish. Have you transport or shall I send a car round for you?"

Assuming a country-house confidence, Upshaw said, "They usually have two or three here, I'll borrow one." His personal driver's license had not been taken away from him. He thought about the cars in the garage and decided on the dark red Mercedes. A kind of wrap-up secret joke, driving himself to Dunragh Castle in Paul Kinsella's Mercedes, which had taken shelter in the garage at Ballybrophy, at Amy Veagh's.

But his clothing? A fresh tie would help a lot. The blue-and-green stripe hadn't been in the best shape when he'd started off from Dublin a world ago, three days ago. He had washed his white shirt last night and it was, if a bit rumpled, nice and clean.

Buoyed up by his invitation and mentally seeing crisp high-denomination bills being counted into Bel Kinsella's hand in Dublin—or would it be a check?—he knocked boldly on the library door and then unbidden went in.

James was trying to concentrate on *Elizabeth and Her German Garden*, which he read at least once a year. *"Luckily I had sown two great patches of sweetpeas, which made me very happy all the summer, and then there were some wallflowers and a few . . ."*

"Sorry to interrupt, but can you lend me a tie? I'm to run over to the castle for lunch."

James concealed his first reaction, which was simple astonishment. He didn't like the idea of any tie of his around Upshaw's neck, but he felt he could hardly refuse.

Admitted to his bedroom, Upshaw selected one of James's favorites, a russet knit with a frosty white fleck in the weave. "This ought to do. In a way dressed up, but nothing too fancy about it."

In a state now approaching distress, James went back to the library. The invitation was obviously grotesque, the idea of Upshaw as Banning's luncheon guest. Banning was a snob to his toes. He must intend to use the man in some way. And after the nasty deadline threat in Bel's room, and her flight to Dublin to close an evil box, he thought there was only one center, one core, to this peculiar little mealtime plot.

Banning, in some unknowable way at the moment, presented himself as a part of whatever was happening to Bel.

Not being allowed to drive would hardly apply to the mile and a quarter by road to Dunragh. But let Upshaw precede him by ten minutes or so. *If,* in this time of dark swimming uncertainties, he was actually going to Dunragh.

They must have a cozier place somewhere here to eat, Upshaw thought, when just the two of them are at home. But nevertheless he was pleased with the enormous dining room. Great heavily gilded pieces, lion-footed, against the paneled pale green walls—or was that real gold on them? Fourteen-foot windows hung in thick green-and-white striped stuff; he imagined the price of the yardage alone would keep him in comfort for months. A vast white cabinet affair with a burglar's wild dream of treasure on its shelves. At one end of the shining sweep of the mahogany table two places were laid, on frail lace-and-linen mats, a lighted candle at each.

And, cheering sight, *three* wine glasses at each.

He had hoped the General would be present to add the final touch of glory, but he was nowhere to be seen. "The poor fellow is committeed to death," Banning explained, pouring pre-lunch sherry for both of them in the room where he'd been given his new black shoes. "Takes the welfare of the countryside very much to heart."

Upshaw was at first awed and uncomfortable, unable to think of anything to say. Banning filled the impending silences with bursts of chatter. Mostly incomprehensible to his listener: the goings-on in this morning's *Times* and the *Irish Times*. And, gossipy, the peculiar behavior of Lady Midden, their neighbor on the right, who, Banning thought, must be up to her eyelids in dope day in and day out.

He paused here, and his alert gaze embarrassed Upshaw. Speak up, say something intelligent. "There's a lot of that kind of thing around," he ventured. "But what I suspect is, look where there's money to burn and that's where you'll find it. The less fortunate have to be content with the beer and the whiskey." And then he hoped that Banning would not think he was identifying himself with the great gray mass, the less fortunate of the world.

"I'd call that rather a sweeping generalization—excuse the unintended pun—and now shall we go in?"

Still attempting brisk brightness, response, Upshaw laughed. "Generalization, General, that's good. As they say, present company excepted, don't they?"

He didn't know the names of most of the things they ate and drank and didn't like to ask. Something like a beef broth, but it had a taste of caraway too. A fillet of some kind of fish with a sauce of some kind of cheese. An unfamiliar cut of lamb, probably cost the earth, that's why he'd never had it before, tender inch-thick rounds with fresh asparagus. Tiny strawberries in clotted cream. "Flown in from France, the berries," Banning informed him. "But of course you recognized that odd flowery flavor."

And wine. White, followed by a deep rich red with the lamb and a rosé with the strawberries. His glass was assiduously refilled by the Vietnamese servingman.

"Let's have coffee and brandy in my little snug, shall we?" Banning asked, crumpling his splendid linen damask napkin.

Upshaw, feeling delightfully blurred, and as though flooded inside by sunshine on this dark rain-soaked day, said that would be nice, very nice.

Bel's black Mini, which she used for local runs, was light and easy to drive. Think of it as a sort of bicycle, James told himself, hardly a car at all.

The Dunragh gate was open. Partway down the drive, he took the left fork that circled to the garage and stables and guest cottages. He put the Mini behind one of the cottages and approached the rear of the long golden-gray building.

Pleasantly humble domestic touch: a fresh-faced girl was just heaving soapy water from a doorway onto the cobblestones of the courtyard. She had obviously been scrubbing the stone passageway that led past the flower room. James knew the castle well. In his youth, he had been an ardent amateur photographer, and when visiting Leam had found the great empty crumbling place, with its shafts of light and leaf-whispering shadows, full of fascinating subjects for his Rolleiflex.

He knew the girl with the pail. A year or so back she had helped out Mrs. Broth when there were ten or more to dinner. He went over to her in his hesitant courteous way and when she smiled and ducked her head at him, said, "I want to surprise Mr. Banning. I'll just slip in past you. You haven't seen me at all."

"I'm just after setting out my lunch in there, and coffee and brandy was ordered for his office," the girl volunteered. "And how is everybody at the house, sir? Nice to see you, Mr. Kinsella."

"Is there anyone in the kitchen now? I don't want to leak my surprise."

"You'll be best off using the back staircase—ours—just before you come to the kitchen. His office is on the second floor toward the front. I'll go in and make a commotion for you and cover any sound. And isn't it awful about"—seeming hardly able to speak the dead disgraced name—"Agnes?"

"Frightful," James said, feeling a pinch of shame because in his searing worry about Bel the fact of the girl's death had almost slipped his mind.

Quietly, he made his way up the stone-encased stairs. If he met anyone, a servant, he'd say—what? But nothing to worry about, he was a respectable country gentleman. He'd laugh and say he'd lost his way.

He met no one.

Upshaw, who associated the word office with tiny cubbyholes crammed with papers and battered wooden furniture, was very much impressed with Banning's office, his "little snug." No brocades or damasks or gold, but everything white and dark blue, including the furniture. Not a paper in sight.

A coffee tray was placed by the Vietnamese on the round table in front of the great fat white sofa. Upshaw hoped that the seat of his pants, his suit not overclean, wouldn't mark the white cushion.

They drank their coffee and double brandies and then Banning said, "Now to business. Suppose we conduct it over here."

He sat down on one side of a shining lacquered dark blue slab desk and gestured Upshaw into the straight chair across from him.

What business? The jovial, hostly look was gone. Banning reached into his breast pocket and put on a pair of black-rimmed glasses, which somehow made his skin look paler.

Obediently, Upshaw sat down facing him, hands planted on his knees. Was the man thinking of offering him work of some sort? But that didn't fit with all the wine, and the food, and the ceremony.

"How much?" Banning asked. His voice was different too, at once harsh and very quiet.

Upshaw blinked. He knew immediately he didn't like the sound of the two words.

"How much what?"

"You really don't know what I'm talking about?"

Upshaw felt a little dizzy and his ears were ringing. All right, too much to drink; but drink didn't explain what Banning was saying, or asking.

"No, I don't."

Banning got up from his chair and went to a wall cabinet. Opening it, he took out a gun, black, shining, with an eight-inch barrel. He sat down again before the frozen gaze of his guest and pulled out a drawer. From it he took a manila folder, the face of which he held outward for Upshaw to see. On it was a neatly typed label, "Upshaw, John."

He laid the folder on the desk and put the gun on top of it.

"For the last time," he said. "How much? To spell it out since you seem struck dumb—how much for the business you're here on? What is the sum that will send you quietly on your way so that we shall have an end, permanently, of John Upshaw in the vicinity of Leam?"

Oh Jesus, who'd ever believe it? Upshaw asked himself. And he thinking Mrs. K. had gone to get the money for him. Now it seemed apparent that the transaction was in this neighbor's hands.

He found himself frightened, sweating. Get it over with, get out of here. Speak up, man.

"Ten thousand pounds," he said. His throat had gone dry and there was a croaking sound to his voice.

Banning silently got out a checkbook and wrote a check. Holding it by one corner, he said, "You of course plan to leave today."

"Well, yes, now that—" James's tie must be returned to him. "Of course I'll have to go back and say good-bye. It would look funny if I didn't. And, collect my things." The last an attempted summoning of some sort of dignity. It felt peculiar to be treated this way, handed this money, with no emotion at all. With no show of anger, no resentment. Strictly business.

He folded the check and put it in his pocket and stood up.

"You can find your own way out, I assume." Banning picked up the gun. "And do bear this in mind, always."

Upshaw went to the door and opened it. Euphoria caught him in a rising wave. No matter how nasty it had been, he had his money. Turning in the doorway, he said, "And to think I thought it would be from the hand of Mrs. Kinsella. If I don't see her before I go, will you thank her for me?" The sight of the gun made his skin prickle at his fingertips. "And tell her I won't be back again. Tell her Paul Kinsella is safe and sound in his grave."

Sixteen

Wanting some air to breathe—there didn't seem to be any of it in the room—Banning went to the window and flung it up so hard that one of the panes cracked.

He only half heard himself punctuating obscenities with blasphemies, followed by, "Oh dear, dear me, now what will I—?"

His telephone on the desk rang. It was, horribly enough, Nou. As though the man from a distance of forty-five miles had heard every word just spoken in this room.

Nou had left at eleven to attend a meeting of Mrs. Caveppowell's Society of Geraniums. The great present goal of the Society was to develop a yellow geranium. Nou's gardener had come close with a new, pale orange, and his master went off triumphantly with the precious pot.

"Everything in train?" Nou asked.

Oh Christ yes, but the train's going in the wrong direction, and at top speed.

"Yes," Banning said. Their telephone conversations were of necessity laundered.

"Everything?"

What would happen if he wasn't on top, or seen later to have been not on top, of everything?

Banning had seldom known personal fear: one's own cherished heart-beating breathing self at stake. The point of the blade at the shrinking mortal breast. *One thrust—*

"Yes. Everything."

He went back to the window, hands clasped tightly behind his back and shoulders braced. Seeing without seeing it, he watched the dark red Mercedes going away, down the drive. The man in it with a check for ten thousand pounds, the wrong check for the wrong thing, in his pocket.

The high window commanded the place where the drive split to send one long circling arm to the rear of the castle. Along this arm came a familiar black Mini. It concealed itself from the main driveway for a minute or two on the other side of the rhododendron hedge. Then, when the Mercedes passed the split, it very cautiously started to move again. Banning darted for his field glasses and got a close-up of James Kinsella's naked stricken face.

The Mini followed the Mercedes, about forty feet behind.

Now what have I got here? Banning's mind moved with computer speed. Yes. That mind-blasting last statement of Upshaw's. James here, uninvited, he'd have to have followed the invited guest. James listening, somewhere near, to the voices in the office. Especially to Upshaw's voice, departing? James who had obviously loved his brother and to the instructed eye just as obviously adored Bel Kinsella.

James's admirable Jermyn Street tie around Upshaw's neck.

Now don't panic. Or perhaps, old son, *do* panic. That's what sends the juices of awful necessity hotly through your veins and arteries. The improbable and near impossible might work, if you got right at it under this whip. Had to—yes again, keep the invigorating frenzy ablaze—had to work.

What I might just have here, concluded Banning to himself, is salvation.

"A sad loss, a nice young fellow, I'll miss him at McCane's," Mrs. Broth said to Mrs. McNooth in Wishy Gorman's crowded cottage. And then lowering her voice, "This ham's a bit on the tough side."

It was close to noon on that now legendary day in Leam.

All through the mass, and at the cemetery, she had felt at least two feet off the ground, insecurely floating in rosy air. "Salary fifteen thousand pounds."

But *was* it a joke? Sara Parry laughing when she snatched away the plate of Tidbits for hungry Mr. Mamood. "Never mind, he'll probably want to purchase you." But Sara was a nice young woman, soft and mannerly; surely that wouldn't be her idea of fun?

"Fully paid hospital service for life." What a fool she'd look if she sent off a cablegram accepting a nonexistent offer. And anyway did she really want to leave Leam and the Kinsellas for hot foreign parts where the air was no doubt thick with sinister germs?

She was fond of Fitz and Mrs. Kinsella, and she had a reverent love for James. Could she bear to say good-bye to James forever? Mr. Mamood seemed to have establishments pretty well everywhere, except in Ireland.

Let it wait. There were a dozen things wanting to be done when she got back to the house, what with Fitz's birthday, always a bustling celebration. And it would look more dignified to let a day or so pass before she answered. *If* it was real. *If* it was true.

Sara had had a bad night. Hearing in one terrible dream Agnes Morley calling to her from behind a high wall and she trying to scale it, rope burning her palms. And then—the worse because it seemed a kind of frivolity in the light of the girl's death—Conor and Fitz switching images. At one point, Fitz's mouth on hers; but the sweet known hand stroking her breast was Conor's.

If only he had not come, she felt, knew, that this day, old and tired and dark now at four o'clock, Fitz's birthday, would have been a final one for both of them. "Put on something festive for me," he had said to her yesterday evening. "Not that you don't always look like a morning full of birds. It might be wise to prepare yourself for a dramatic announcement to the assembled company."

Well, why not? Conor had staked no formal claim, only dropped back into her life like a thunderbolt. "My once," ticked the clock, "and future Sara." An articulate man, like his cousin: nice words. But nice words came easily to Conor. A sort of jealousy—Fitz not allowed to have his former girl? A dog-in-the-manger rivalry of kindred blood? Spoil it, scrub it, and then merrily off on his way. "Well, I fixed that for good and all."

If she had left here, as she had intended to, things might have straightened themselves out in her head. No matter what Conor said about packing your troubles in your suitcase, you could sometimes get a perspective from a cool objective distance. Conor, a love past and put away, flaring up inside her, affecting her vision, her judgment. But it was he who had stopped her from going away, she wasn't quite sure how or why.

Was it, perhaps, his open assumption, while putting her clothes back in the closet, that she was his? And was she to be labeled as his for the rest of their lives, or for destroying years of hers, while they pursued their separate courses?

She fell into the deep morning sleep a bad night offers as the only palliative to its endless white hours. She got up late, to a buzz of silent unanswered questions in the air about her. Pay attention to the little, daily things. Light the fire, make coffee, have a long hot bath. While that poor Gorman boy was being prayed over and put into his grave. Dress now, or you won't want to make the effort later; or you may begin to think about running away again. Not the white, *not* wedding white. Would she be able to stop him before he got the words out to the assembled company? Would she want to?

And not black, for God's sake. Her hyacinth-colored thin wool would do, a shirt dress but it had cost a fortune and looked it. The rakish flicked-up collar took long looped pearls nicely; her grandmother's pearls. Fitz wouldn't know their origin, wouldn't know they were special, couldn't take them as any sort of promise in advance.

There was a light owning knock at the door. Fitz. Opening it, he bent and picked up a white envelope which had been half slipped in underneath.

He was fresh from an informal opening-gun party at the stables, where the staff of eight, with the mysterious exception of Trahey, had mixed him up an immense punchbowl of brandy-cup and joyfully prepared to share it with him. This beverage was made of equal portions of champagne and brandy with several bottles of Guinness to further enrich and froth it. His health was drunk and drunk again, his many happy returns summoned for future decades.

He's just a little rosy, Sara thought, feeling apprehensive; not over the edge at all. Fitz was a marvel at handling his liquor.

"Have you had breakfast? Shall I fix you some?"

"I shall breakfast on you," Fitz said, close, bending to kiss her. "Frightful when you think of it to celebrate while someone is being buried, but it does remind you that life is short." The kiss was light, a delicate pre-tasting. "And I suppose," he added against her forehead, "every sweetest moment of one's existence is someone else's sad or sour or awful moment at the identical clock-tick. And vice versa."

She wasn't prepared for an all-out love scene. Just the two of us, who may or may not be going to be married. "What's that you picked up off the floor?"

"Oh—I forgot it." He took the letter out of his pocket and turned it over. On its face was written, in Conor's stylish black scrawl, "To Sara in a hurry."

He looked from the envelope to her face and then backed away from her, three paces. In the silence, she heard a distant bark from Peach, and the rain against the panes.

"Well, give it to me, Fitz, if it's something in a hurry."

"I will," Fitz said. "Aloud. It might answer some questions for both of us."

He opened the envelope with his pen knife. She saw in his hand one closely covered folded sheet.

" 'Sara darling.' " He read the two words and then stopped. Unreal, ghastly. His voice had somewhat the sound of Conor's.

"Obviously not an open letter," she managed, her breathing constricted. "Do give it here."

" 'Sara darling, Our race has a certain love for drama and is inclined to make large decisions on marked days. Next Monday I will go on the wagon. On Ash Wednesday I will for six weeks drop four-letter words from my vocabulary. On his birthday, I will say, yes, Fitz, why not. Please don't say it, Sara, at least not today, at least not until we can talk.' "

The lines from Fitz's nose to his mouth corners had deepened and were, oddly, not shadowed but white against the skin reddened by weather and brandy-cup.

"Fitz, *don't*."

" 'I would have called you this morning but I was and am occupied, and anyway certain things, like commitment, look firmer somehow on paper. And you managed to make yourself incommunicado last night. Where were you? Don't you know that when I don't know where you are my right hand, or left foot, or one of my eyes, seems to have been mislaid, always has and now again always will.' "

" 'Always has,' " Fitz repeated thoughtfully. "When did always start, Sara?" He was perfectly still but there was a throbbing in the room.

She should be angry at this outrageous breach of privacy, but she could only feel wretched. And something deep under the wretchedness, a leaping, a flickering butterflied warmth.

"For God's sake, Fitz, in this day and age prospective lovers don't supply each other with typed lists and descriptions of other encounters they have had, or she, or I"—stumbling a little—"in my twenty-eight years on this sinful earth."

"Which means you and he happily bedded down together, of course. Well, to proceed. 'I don't think a roving life will bother you too much, yours is a portable profession. And I've reason to think we might be centered in Paris in four months or so. You can gather from these calculations that—' I don't want to hear the rest, do you? Wordy fellow for someone in a hurry." He balled the letter in his fist and threw it into the fire.

Slowly, carefully, he moved toward her. She had never heard his voice sound the way it did now: metallic but molten.

"If you're a free-for-all, and as it's my birthday, suppose I help myself to my share." There wasn't, now, passion in the grip of his arms and the explicit embrace of his body, but a rage to shiver the surface of the skin.

Fighting, Sara gasped, "As he said, our race has a love for drama—*no—Fitz*—"

There was a double rap at the door and then at the window beside it a face under a large brown feathered hat. "Yoohoo!" called Mrs. Broth cheerfully.

"Oh Christ." Fitz dropped his arms and she saw that he was shaking. From him, an almost apocalyptic word; he never in her hearing had allowed himself to drop into blasphemy.

"Let her in," he said, his voice sounding exhausted. "I must have a word with her before I leave here."

"Hope I didn't interrupt breakfast or anything," Mrs. Broth said, closing her umbrella and shaking it out over the doorstep. "It's just that I wanted to have a word with Sara. About a cablegram I got this morning."

Fitz picked up his raincoat. "As soon as you get back to the house, will you please do this. Pack everything of Conor's and put the bag in the hall. Everything. He's leaving, and when he goes it will be in a great hurry. And I mean, Mrs. Broth, within the next fifteen minutes, the packing."

"Mother in heaven," Mrs. Broth said as the door closed behind him. "And on his birthday too, what's got into him? I'd better hurry then—Sara, you didn't send me a cablegram for fun, about that man Mr. Mamood?"

Sara looked at her as if she either hadn't heard the question or couldn't believe she had heard it. "A cable? For fun? No."

"Well, I just thought I'd ask. I'd better be off. It's not his house, not yet, but every so often, once or twice a year, he's a hard man to stand up to. Temper. His grandfather's I'm told."

In the room still echoing with near violence and crackling rage, Sara went to the fireplace. It would have been nice if she could have read, or—no, not heard from those other lips—the rest of Conor's letter. But there was nothing left of it. It had been thrown into the heart of the fire.

"We have plenty of everything?" Conor asked Ike, on the way to Kilkieran Bay.

"Besides film, you mean? Yes. Food, drink, bedding for anyone who wants a nap. And a—to drop into the language of the country —a bit of a gun."

He gave Conor a long sharp dark look. He was half smiling. "It seemed a necessary item up there in Belfast with other people's bullets whizzing around, and some of them didn't exactly take to the camera. I don't believe we'll need it here in the peaceful south. Or west, or wherever we are."

Their driver was named Kit Donahue. While assigned to the wheel, he was in the process of learning the television trade. As a start, he had grown a thorny red beard, and wore rough dirty denims and heeled creaking leather ankle boots. He seemed somewhat taken aback by Conor's clean-shaven jaw and English trench coat and throwaway air of a gentleman of leisure, brushed and fresh to his well-trimmed fingernails.

"Ilch first, I think," Conor said, remembering the pocket of loud silence in the bar when Upshaw had inquired about the *Mary Jean*.

Asked afterward about his intentions concerning the filming, he said he was just stirring snakes with a stick. Or dropping a stone

into a pond to see how many ripples it would make. And you'll re-
alize, my dear sirs, that in case there *was* something, the film itself
would turn out to be a valuable property as far as international
news coverage went. He left out two basic reasons. His reporter's
instinct, drive, to find out, to know. And the probability that if he
just left it, and went away, Wishy Gorman and more especially
Agnes Morley would lie in their graves forever unspoken for.

It was Fair Day in Ilch, the town a jostle and hum of buying
and selling, the roads, as they had been from dawn, full of the pat-
tering of hooves. The men were muddy and the cattle were wet.
Drivers resignedly picked their way around them, or sought back
lanes, or gave up the whole business and headed for the handiest
pub.

Ike, with the pleasure of one brought up in a near-slum in New
York, shot footage to his heart's content. The big red bullocks, the
biscuit-colored Jerseys, the black Kerrys. "Why has that white
cow got a red rag tied to her tail?" he asked. "To avert the evil
eye," Conor told him.

By coincidence or not, a good portion of the fishing fleet was in,
rocking in the rain. Conor, not wanting to thrust Upshaw's lines
on Ike, shouted while at the docks once, twice, three times—"Has
anyone seen the *Mary Jean?*"

The van was parked at the mouth of one of the piers, the camera dollied out, the cables causing a good deal of side-stepping of
fish-scaled rubber boots.

"A view of the town and the bay from the hills, I think," Conor
said after they had had a pint at the Kestrel's Rest. "Then on to
Kilkieran."

Donahue parked the van facing downhill in a narrow cobblestoned lane between rows of color-washed houses. There was another pub just above, and the lane was busy. Donahue remained at
the wheel while the other two got out and got to work.

A small boy ran up the lane and looked in at the driver's window. "They say you'd better get right out of the van," he called.
"They say it's life and death." And then he vanished into a narrow
aperture between a rose house and a yellow house.

Donahue, fresh from Belfast, flung open the door and ducked
rapidly into the same aperture.

Around Conor and Ike, there was a small crowd gathering.

Children and adults and three donkeys. There was a sudden clatter as a piebald horse was ridden down the hill at show-off speed. A cry of, "Look out for the devil on horseback," and laughter, and then, from somewhere a little higher up the hill, from a doorway or window where the little lane angled sharply to the left, a flung object, its passage through the air barely visible.

The back of the van was open, with its ramp down. In a tremendous *whump* and a flare of orange, and filthy blue smoke, the van seemed to fly to pieces.

"Oh Christ, all my film! I just loaded a reel," Conor heard Ike say amid the screaming and shouting.

The piebald's rackety dash had forced the onlookers to the left of the lane and the bottle-bomb, while accurately thrown, had hit slightly to the right inside. There were, it turned out later, few injuries to flesh or property. A child's thumb cut with flying glass, a woman's bunned hair ripped loose and flowing when a shard of metal neatly undid the hairpins; broken windows in the lower floors of three houses.

A police whistle sounded from up the hill and from the bottom of the lane the hooter of a fire engine. Conor felt a sharp pain where something had struck him behind the hipbone, but he didn't pause to investigate. Police, inquiries, hours of detention, and explanation, immobilized fifty miles away from Leam—

The snake in the somnolent pile had waked, hissed, reared its head and struck, with death in its fangs.

"Take care of it, will you? The police and so on. I'll see you at Leam." And before Ike could stop him he had slipped between the rose house and the yellow one and into the next lane, and began to run downhill. Forty yards up the bay road from the Kestrel's Rest he remembered a small car-hire yard. Pausing for a moment before the little wooden box of an office at its entrance, he lifted his jacket flap and saw blood where his shirt met his belt. Better get off and away before he was openly dripping, they wouldn't want their car stained.

The only one available was an old, small black Ford. "She wants a bit of understanding, but with kindly treatment she'll get you from Malin Head to Bantry and back again like a trojan," the car-hire man said, filling the gas tank.

He drove fast and thought hard. If he had expected something immediate, concrete, it was a forbidding arm going up: get the hell away from here with that damned camera. Then a report from him to Grady, with just a cautious hint or two. It might be worthwhile, Sergeant Grady, to see why they didn't want the (man, building, boat) photographed. It would be nothing new to him, an attempt even to smash the camera.

But this daring, swift and skillful all-out move—was it lives Banning was after, or film already accumulated? He no longer substituted whoevers for Banning; too much trouble, and it was too late. Banning couldn't know how much he had guessed or gathered about the drug operation. He, Conor, might by knowledge or accident zero in on the one or two things or people or places that must not be known or questioned or searched until— Until what? Until a place, perhaps a collecting and dispatching center, was emptied. Until a boat was safely unloaded. Until a man had been given warning and had a cloak of words to wrap around him.

To destroy the film was one thing. But there was still a dangerous man around nosing into other people's business. What did you do about Conor Niall, who might be infuriated but not terrified into flight by an exploding van?

Get at him, one way or another. (A random half-recollection surfaced—had he or hadn't he seen Trahey's flat yellow head at a window up the hill just before the explosion? *Trahey?*)

Get at him, as it seemed increasingly clear Wishy Gorman and Agnes Morley had been gotten at. But a *third* body? And an American? Inconvenient. Put some kind of pressure on him—

He had thought his way full circle back to what had sent him tearing off down the hill at Ilch. Sara.

What a nice hostage Sara would make, to shut him up permanently.

And if not Sara, something or someone else close to him, some lethal way to control him.

Like the billow of orange on the cobblestoned hill, something fast.

Seventeen

Can I or can't I make it to the house? James asked himself, driving very slowly. The Mercedes several hundred yards ahead of him had just turned in at the driveway.

No, I don't think I can. His vision was darkening, and the familiar accelerated fluttering in his breast told him one of his attacks was coming on.

"Tell her Paul Kinsella is safe and sound in his grave."

Don't any longer, for now, think about the words and what they might mean. Save it until he got his firm center back. He stopped the car just inside the gates. He got out and began walking at a prudent pace, one of his capsules under his tongue. Reaching a cluster of silver birches, he sat down and rested for a time against a sturdy bole, pulling his raincoat protectively around him. But the rain on his bare head and face felt cool and refreshing. Mustn't, however, invite a cold, a chill. He got to his feet and thought they would carry him to Sara's cottage with a little effort and a great deal of will.

Even if she wasn't there, the cottage as far as he knew was seldom locked. But she was. He heard, when he got to her door, the sound of her typewriter going at a furious pace.

"I am so sorry, Sara," when the door opened, "I'm interrupting you at work."

"That's all right—*James,* what is it?"

He had reached out a groping hand and she took it in both of hers. "You're cold, you're wet—"

"Just one of my little spells," James said from a dimming place far from her. "If I might just lie down on your sofa for a bit."

She led him there, rearranged cushions, brought a plaid throw and tenderly tucked it in around him. "I won't flutter and peck, but, doctor or not?"

"No doctor. I've had my medicine, just rest. I'll be quite all right, I always have been before," James assured her, unaware that his words could just barely be heard. A blessed warmth, peace, unknowingness came to him as he let the darkness fall, now that it was safe to allow it to take over.

When he woke, he thought that he had been out, or asleep, for about an hour. It had been one-thirty on his watch when he left Dunragh on Upshaw's heels. The first thing he saw was Sara, sitting near him in her slipper chair, intent green eyes on him.

She had had a frightening time. She debated calling the doctor no matter what James's expressed wish was. But then she thought that with the telephone not six feet from his head, the sounds of the call, the commotion when the doctor came, might do him more harm than good. He was an intelligent man, James. He would not wave away medical help if he thought it was at all necessary. *But.* And she didn't like the idea of leaving him alone, going over to the other house to use the phone.

It had been a great relief to see the pink color coming slowly back to his skin. Alarming at first to find how much younger, unlined, innocent his sleeping face looked. But perhaps James always looked that way when he was asleep.

Blue eyes open, he smiled at her. "What a nice quiet presence to find at one's side. And what a nuisance I've been."

"Tea or brandy or both, James dear?"

"Both. You probably haven't even been able to use your typewriter, afraid of waking me." He sat up experimentally and lowered his still damply trousered legs. Then his palm flew to his cheek as memory came rushing back.

Handing him a little glass of brandy, she said, "What—? James, do lie back again. I am going to call the doctor no matter what you say."

"No, I'm all right." He drank off his brandy in two swallows. "I just remembered something I must attend to. I'll be a bit rubber-legged for a short time, will you do me a favor?"

"Yes, of course."

"I think Upshaw's planning to leave, and I must speak to him before he goes. Will you—you're probably going over soon anyway —keep an eye on him for me? Don't let him slip away."

Sara, who had other pressing concerns on her mind, thought only that James was planning to give Upshaw a farewell check.

"Another hour on your sofa should put me back in perfect running order." Gratefully accepting his tea and hot buttered toast, "Don't worry about me, I'll read." And try not to think, not yet. "Do I see Colette's book of flowers over in the bookcase?"

She would have had to turn up, sooner or later, to hand the present and wish happy birthday, but right now it was extremely difficult to face. She put on a very light armor of Chanel Number 22 and makeup, found an umbrella in the closet, kissed James good-bye, and went out and across the bridge.

Would Fitz throw her out too? As he had commanded Conor in absentia to quit these premises?

As it turned out, she needn't have worried about being thrown smack into his company, face to face. Good heavens, they really laid it on, the Heir's Birthday at Leam House. Candles and fires lit, curtains drawn against the rain. The long buffet in the dining room spread end to end with elaborate and beautiful things to eat. Two of Mrs. Broth's cleaning-crew girls demurely aproned for serving. Music playing from the library, warm and sensuous, Offenbach's "Gaietie Parisienne." And people eating, drinking, talking, laughing.

Three sisters in tweeds, jolly red faces, straight whiskies in hand. Lady Midden, tall and green-pale, General Nou's neighbor, with a magnificent white Russian wolfhound she proposed to give Fitz as a present. "I've three more of them, I can easily spare this one." "No thank you, Millicent," Fitz said. "Vesper doesn't take kindly to wolfhounds of other nationalities. Come and have some champagne." Two young men of Fitz's age, who had driven from Dublin for the occasion, a gallery proprietor, an editor in a publishing house. A handsome shaggy playwright from Screeb who, having met Sara once before, headed immediately for her to tell her what a horrible time he was having with his second act.

Presents lying about, on chairs, on the mantelpiece in the drawing room, boxes and tissue and ribbon. Perhaps the one unfestive note, Upshaw standing uneasily all alone in the hall, and right beside him a suitcase, but not his. Conor's, strapped and buckled and ready for departure.

On his return to the house from Dunragh, he had a peculiar feeling of having taken a great jump into nowhere. He was finished with his business here. Time to go. Just collect his things, as he had told Calvin Banning. What things? He had nothing, not even a toothbrush; he'd made do with a busily scrubbing forefinger. Oh yes, he'd left his pocket comb in the bathroom. And just check, to see if there might be bits and pieces of him lying about in that narrow little bedroom. A handkerchief, perhaps, or an opened pack of cigarettes.

None of the people around seemed to take any notice of him as he went up the stairs. He did find a handkerchief, but otherwise the room was as neat, as empty, as though he had never for a few days occupied it.

His eye caught, hooked over the doorknob, his old, his only tie. It looked much more scruffy than he remembered it. He decided to make off, no apologies, with James's handsome russet wool. It wouldn't do to enter on a new life, a prosperous life, wearing a shabby stained tie.

As he stood looking down at the bed a great drowsiness hit him. All that wine— It wouldn't hurt to lie down for a little until his head was clearer.

Stretching out without even troubling to take off his shoes or his suit jacket, he sank into sleep. He woke half an hour later and went on uncertain feet into the bathroom for a last wash-up. The effect of the wine seemed to have gathered, not lost its strength. I'm not drunk, he assured himself anxiously, but I can't call myself sober either.

Looking out the window he saw Trahey, aimlessly strolling, hands in his pockets. Or, not strolling—circling the house, watching it? Watching for him?

But he had said twenty-four hours, and it wasn't that yet. What time had it happened, Trahey and his pitchfork? About a quarter to six. Of course, *he'd* been drunk then, perhaps he had forgotten the exact hour.

I'm not leaving here, Upshaw assured the man in the mirror, without an escort to see me safely away. Who?

Unable at the moment to make any plan he went downstairs again. People around; no one could do you mortal harm in front of onlookers.

Sara saw him standing at the foot of the stairs, looking out of place, lost. She felt a certain sympathy for him as she felt a bit lost herself, not yet having had any confrontation with Fitz. She had left his wrapped present with the other boxes on the mantelpiece, overly extravagant in the light of right now. A set of Trollope's Parliamentary series, bound in gold-tooled curry-colored leather.

Going over to him, she said, "Why don't you get yourself a drink? You aren't rushing anywhere, are you? James wants to see you a little later."

"Did I hear James?" Calvin Banning asked, behind her. "As a matter of fact I was a bit worried—I saw his car, or Bel's rather, parked just inside the gate, no one in it, I couldn't think what it was doing there. I'd thought he wasn't supposed to drive."

"One of his attacks," Sara said. "He's at the cottage."

"Oh—doctor with him?"

"No, resting, he swears he'll be fine in an hour or so, and he did look ninety-three per cent better when I left him. He's tucked up reading Colette."

Seeing Fitz approaching, a suddenly unsmiling Fitz, she turned in a cowardly fashion and fell into conversation with Mavis Gracie, one of the jolly tweeded women, and never after remembered what they had talked about.

"Glad to have caught you before you left," Banning murmured to Upshaw. "Made a bit of a booboo in my haste. I gave you a check on the wrong bank. I don't want to hold you up while funds are being transferred—I'll just write you a new one. You've got the other check handy?"

"Yes," Upshaw said, not quite liking the sound of this. But for all he knew Banning might operate out of a dozen bank accounts.

"Mustn't be seen exchanging checks here, considering the nature of the transaction—" Raising his voice, "Ah, Fitz! Felicitations on this happy day. Bel not here?"

"She's on some mysterious mission to Dublin. But back this evening."

The man's a perfect walking pillar of rage about something, Banning thought. Oh well, get on with it, a check to take care of. "I'll meet you . . . where? . . . in James's greenhouse in ten minutes. I must just have a short chat with Lady Mary."

Upshaw considered for a moment. Trahey hadn't his pitchfork

with him, and he could make a dash for the greenhouse. "All right. And then will you see me safely off the property? Or"—hastily—"or, rather drive me to the bus stop in Costelloe?"

"Glad to," said Banning. "Now to circulate." He did a little drifting and conversing on his way to the kitchen. Mrs. Broth was sitting at the table eating a Tidbit. "Must run down to the stables," he told her. "Mind if I use your kitchen door? The General wants me to take a close look again at Glenquin."

"You're lucky if by now they can form a syllable. Not the horses, I mean, the boys. You wouldn't have sent a cablegram to this house, would you?"

"No, I'd have to have left the country to do that. Lovely party it's being, you do things so well. Hate to leave it."

He made a swift trip to the stables, where he registered his presence on the dazed eyes of one of the Coney brothers. Then around the outer rim of the pool, through the beeches, to James's greenhouse.

"God almighty and all the saints!" The Screeb playwright was on his fifth whiskey and just saved himself from falling as he tripped over the suitcase by the door. Fitz put out a hand to help and then righted the leather case. As he did so a folded note fell to the floor.

He picked it up and read it. "Conor—you can bring your bag over to the cottage when you get back. I think it will be more at home there. Sara."

She was nearby, talking to Peter Devlin, the gallery owner. Fitz's eyes met hers as he bent to put the note back under the strap. Her head fell slowly forward, the soft fair bell of hair swinging to help shield her face.

He went over to her. "It's all happened for the best, hasn't it, darling. Suppose he'd turned up the day after we were married?"

"Fitz. I'm sorry."

"We would both have been sorrier in that case, wouldn't we?"

"What's all this in aid of?" Peter Devlin asked.

"Just a game Sara and I were playing. She was rehearsing for something, and I made an excellent stand-in."

Not wanting to look at his face, Sara looked instead at Upshaw taking an umbrella from the Meissen porcelain cylinder beside the door. "You're not leaving?" she called. "Remember, James wants you."

"Just nipping out to the greenhouse." The more he thought about it the less Upshaw wanted to wait for an interview with James. What if there was some sort of plot now that he had the check on him, James holding him in talk until the Garda came in through the french windows or out from behind the curtains?

Conor managed the journey from the garage to the kitchen, across the bridge, walking slowly. He had stopped a little past Screeb and taken off his shirt and tied it by the sleeves hard and tight over the deep gash, but blood was running into his right shoe and dripping on the ground.

Mrs. Broth uttered a small shriek at the sight of him. "I didn't want to bleed all over your parquet and rugs so I came in this way. Where's Sara?" But he knew at once there was no catastrophe here besides the minor one he had brought in on his body. Thankfully, he allowed himself to collapse on a chair at the table. "I'm not as bad as I look—call a doctor, will you? Is there anyone but that man Quin?"

"Sara's here helping drink up the champagne. There's no other doctor near, Quin it must be." Mrs. Broth put in the call and then brought him half a tumbler of brandy. "You won't bleed to death on me while we wait?"

"No, but I could use a hunk of cotton batting or whatever it is. There's the infection to worry about though. I suppose Quin can fill and empty a hypodermic."

He was dizzy and his voice sounded to him as if it were coming from somebody else's mouth. The brandy began immediately to help.

"This is no time to tell you," Mrs. Broth said, "but it seems you were to leave the house. Fitz's orders. Your bag's all packed, it's in the front hall. With the shape of you, you'll be staying now unless they take you off on a stretcher."

This made no sense whatever to Conor, and he decided to jump over it. "Go and get Sara for me, please. I need sweet sympathy and you seem to be somewhat lacking in it."

"It's just that I have so much on my mind." She corrected this.

"On my hands, rather, dinner to start, ten of them staying. All right, Sara it is."

When she came back to say she couldn't find her, she shrieked again at the sight of his body on the floor.

"Greenhouse, did that little man say?" Mavis Gracie asked. "That reminds me. James and I are having a race with our arum lilies. He claims his are now taller than mine. Just wait while I get my bag, I have a tape measure in it for that express purpose."

Returning with it, she took Sara's arm. "Come along and be a witness that I measured fairly, to the last quarter-inch. Any two umbrellas will suit."

Sara was glad to accompany her. She couldn't imagine any reason why Upshaw should interest himself in hothouse greenery. Had he, after all, been leaving? James was not an asker of favors and he had sounded anxious about this one.

"Blast the rain," Mavis said, setting a hearty pace across the bridge. "But my roses love it. I'm going to put it flatly to James that his Gloire de Dijon can't hold a candle to mine, size of the blossoms that is."

The greenhouse was a large one, L-shaped. Mavis pushed open the door, Sara behind her. "Lilies at the far end, last I saw them. Watch out for that hanging basket." Digging in her bag for her tape measure, she strode purposefully down the crushed pebble path to the right of the trestle tables in the center laden with planters. Then she turned the corner.

"Stop that at once!" she bellowed. Calvin Banning was on one knee beside a man face down and motionless on the pebbles. The man's head was twisted away from her and his tie for some reason was untied and on backward, the ends trailing on the path. In stilled, stretched time, she thought, But that's the tie I gave James last Christmas.

Banning shot to his feet. "I found him just now, dead—strangled," he said. "Quick, for Christ's sake, other door, James is there outside this one, the man's mad—"

Mavis turned, and with him at her heels gasped to Sara, rounding the corner, "Hurry—outside—*run*." Sara reached the door first and flung it open. Banning, between them, seized both their hands and impelled them powerfully forward.

He was a tall, strong man. It was like being attached to a projectile. Sara felt as if her feet were barely touching the ground. Running, gathering greater impetus with every step, down the slope toward the—

She tried without success to wrench her arm away.

Banning slowed two feet from the grassy edge and with an immense heave of his body flung Mavis Gracie out into the water. Then before the stunned Sara could move he picked her up bodily and hurled her in too, and turned and ran.

The pond shelved at its house edges, but here at the outer rim it was abruptly deep, nine feet or so. Surfacing, Sara saw a wild flailing nearby, a head emerging from the water, a convulsed scarlet face. "I can't swim!" screamed Mavis. "Oh God I—" and her head disappeared again. Sara stroked toward her and as she did tried to shout for help. It would be no trick at all for Mavis in her panic to drown both of them.

A gray shape from the bridge flew through the air and hit the water. Vesper. Sara managed to hook one arm under Mavis's chin and had the screaming head above water, against her shoulder. *"Stop stop stop don't kick don't struggle go limp you're all right—"* Vesper fastened his teeth in the billowing silk sleeve of Mavis's dress, not touching the flesh of the wildly thrashing arm under it.

From the open front door of the house, the playwright from Screeb shouted over his shoulder, "Somebody get a gun, quick! There's that great dog in the water savaging two women!"

It was Fitz who came to the rescue, not with panache but safely, dryly, and by then his help was almost not needed. A rope flung to Sara, so that she could haul Mavis more easily to the water's edge.

"Poor dear drowned rats," Fitz said, when they were dripping on the bank, Mavis sitting because her legs wouldn't hold her. "What's this about?"

An audience was gathering around them, Vesper busily shaking his rainstorm over anyone near. Mavis, outraged and quaking with shock, said, "That dreadful man threw us in."

"*What* dreadful man?"

"Banning," Sara offered in a water-choked raw voice.

"Ran us down the slope, supposedly escaping—James couldn't,

he couldn't, but then that was his tie. Is it a joke d'you think, something funny—although I myself don't see the humor of it—for Fitz's birthday?"

"But he said, *dead*." Now, hearing herself taking her turn, Sara thought the two of them sounded like the Madwomen of Chaillot. Scooping back soaked hair from her face and beginning to shiver, she made an effort at coherence. Although coherence would probably sound even madder.

"I didn't see, but I heard. There's a man in the greenhouse dead. Upshaw I suppose. Mavis was ahead of me, apparently she saw Banning—"

"—kneeling beside the body," said Mavis. "I thought he was *doing* something to him. I told him to stop it, but now that I think back his hands were perfectly still."

"Then Banning rushed us out and down the slope. He said to hurry, James was just outside the door at the other end, and that he had just found the body, dead, that is."

"I'll go up to the greenhouse and see if it is a joke," Fitz said. "Peter, will you call the Garda and the doctor while you're at it—Mrs. Broth will have the number. And you two had better get inside before you catch your deaths." He blinked as he uttered the final word.

"And who'll go after Banning?" Sara asked.

"Banning?"

"Well, why else would he throw us in the water? We caught him on the scene and he had to have time to get off it. Of course it's absolute and utter nonsense about James," Sara said.

Banning fled across the bridge and into the woods beyond Sara's cottage. The Dunragh Bentley parked outside the garage would for a bit confuse possible pursuers. The black Volvo was waiting faithfully for him, where he had left it before driving over in the Bentley. Almost hidden under branches in the disused, overgrown bridle path.

A tough car, thank God, bucketing and lurching but making good headway through saplings and over great humps of grass and moss. Reaching the back gates of Dunragh, which he had left open, Banning took a few precious seconds to close them again, then drove across a meadow perilously open to the sky, around a copse of rowan, and into the converted barn where Nou stabled his two helicopters.

As a matter of course, Banning had kept a well-oiled escape hatch open for several years; had, in fact, set up alternates. Take the first. Nou kept a small establishment at Malin Head, the northernmost point of Ireland, for possible emergencies of his own. A thatched cottage, one tenant, an employee of theirs; fitted up with among other things drums of fuel for the helicopters.

Interpol would be looking for him. Yes, continue on to the lonely wild north. The shooting box in Scotland, near Oban on the Firth of Lorne, bought under the name of a William Walker. The fictitious Mr. Walker occasionally entertained Nou as his guest for the grouse in August and September.

Money there, plenty of it. And peace and quiet, and time to change Calvin Banning into another man, of a quite different appearance and accent and style of being.

Nou would know, or guess, where he was. Deal with that when it arose. Yes, General, Upshaw took the check, our greedy little man from Narcotics. Well, you knew he couldn't in any case be allowed to leave Leam alive, but it occurred to me that *three* sad mysterious deaths in a row . . . I've managed to lay this one right in the Kinsellas' lap. There's some trouble in that house, something to do with Bel and the deceased husband. James was actually following Upshaw around. And so on. Yes. Nou had a built-in conviction anyway that most of the Irish were demented.

"And you, my fine fellow, slept through it all," said Walter Tierne, sitting in the bedroom in the big chair beside the window.

"Not slept, fainted," Conor said. "Or I suppose passed out sounds more manly. With a crash on the kitchen floor. Quin got me up the back stairs to bed. He'd barely had me bandaged and needled when all hell broke loose out in front, and he had to go and examine the God-have-mercy corpse."

"Have another drink?" Walter asked. "Yes, poor fellow." Sympathy in his voice, but he looked remarkably collected and cheerful. "Grady downstairs tells me the big boys are on their way from Dublin. No doubt they'll have it all sorted out in no time."

"*Should* you have another drink, Conor?" Sara said from the other chair, where she was becomingly sprawled, in the folds and ripples of white she had hesitated to put on for Fitz. Her eyes met his: sweet green private gaze with something of the wifely in it.

"Yes, why not?" Had he, by putting a question into Upshaw's mouth at Ilch and Kilkieran, been responsible for his death? Impossible. No, possible. But, from the jumble of information he had gotten from Grady in exchange for his own, Upshaw had been invited to a splendid lunch at Dunragh, Banning's guest. Oh God, don't go on thinking the unthinkable until you know what this is all about. In spite of himself, a blitheness began to rise in him. "Quin didn't pull his forelock for me, I think I'll hold up on his bill. Oh well no, we'll be leaving here tomorrow."

Ike Mendelssohn, leaning against the dresser, said, "Like hell you will. There's still stuff we have to cover. I can see this running in, say, three parts on Special Segment, hot as a pistol."

Mrs. Broth knocked and came in with a tray, heavily loaded. "You'll have to make some kind of dent in the birthday food, Conor. Fitz has taken them all off to the Queen. This is no house to have a party meal in, and the Garda have left them all ragged. And thirsty."

She placed the tray on the bedside table. "Mrs. Kinsella says to say she'll see you all later, she's just lying down for a bit. James is with her. Food on the buffet kept hot for those who still have the use of their legs."

In the doorway, she added as an afterthought, "I heard just on the way up the stairs that they picked up that Banning in his plane off Malin Head. One of those Chinese—or, well, you know—at Dunragh passed the hint to them."

Ike said, "I'm hungry, I'll escort you down the stairs, Mrs. Broth."

This seemed to her a heaven-sent opportunity. An American; a man of the world. And Jews were rumored to be notoriously good when it came to matters of business.

"You wouldn't mind bringing your plate into my kitchen? I'd like to ask your advice about a cablegram I've been sent."

Ike read it gravely. "It sounds just fantastic enough to be true," he said, attacking with his knife and fork a thick tender slice of rare roast beef. "Here's my advice to you. Don't sign any contract even if they put lighted matches under your fingernails. Take a year's leave of absence. Then if you don't like the job, come back to Erin, mavourneen."

"Now there's sense for you," cried Mrs. Broth. "And I'll tell you what. I'll put in a contingency to exhibit my independence. I have a foot problem I won't burden you with. But—yes, I'll put in *my* cablegram that it's a condition of my position that while at work I will wear my sneakers."